HOP ALLEY

HOP ALLEY

SCOTT PHILLIPS

COUNTERPOINT
BERKELEY

Library of Congress Cataloging-in-Publication Data

Phillips, Scott, 1961-
Hop Alley : a novel / Scott Phillips.
pages cm
1. Murder—Investigation—Fiction. I. Title.

PS3566.H515H88 2014
813'.54—dc23

2013043962

ISBN 978-1-61902-307-9

Cover design by Michael Fusco
Interior design by Domini Dragoone

COUNTERPOINT
1919 Fifth Street
Berkeley, CA 94710
www.counterpointpress.com

Printed in the United States of America
Distributed by Publishers Group West

10 9 8 7 6 5 4 3 2 1

FOR CORT McMEEL

PROLOGUE

Omaha, Nebraska, November 1873

Maggie was unhappy. Six months with me in the wilderness—proverbial but also, too often, literal—had sapped the joy from her, that delightful *esprit* that had attracted me to her as much as her considerable physical charms. As disastrous and miserable as the summer and fall of 1873 had been, the coming winter augured still worse, and as the weather had begun growing cooler Maggie's normally garrulous and cheerful disposition curdled into an ominous silence, which I feared would end with her walking out on me to take her chances elsewhere.

It was my fault that we had been living in such a rude and penurious manner, crisscrossing the plains and stopping in towns too new or poor to have a permanent photographer, there making stereographic pictures of those few residents who could afford such a luxurious memento. Few of these towns had a boarding house suitable for a woman's custom, and many was the night we slept in a canvas tent camped along a river; we considered ourselves very fortunate when we occasionally obtained permission to sleep in a hayloft stinking of horse piss, bare planks bespeckled with swallow shit.

I knew, too, that she missed the company of other women, for the towns we visited were largely populated by males of the sort who wander the western areas of our country looking for opportunity; seeing Maggie's reaction to these villages I understood that they were unlikely, barring some fantastic stroke of good fortune, to attract many of the softer sex.

AND SO WHEN we arrived at the city of Omaha, Nebraska, I thought to regain some of her favor by checking into the Cozzens House hotel, which was reputed to be the finest in the middle of the nation, despite the town's reputation for roughness, violence, and general squalor. Viewed from a purely economic standpoint this was not the wisest course of action open to me, but I hoped Maggie's spirits would revive once she'd tasted a bit of the *vie de luxe* away from which I'd spirited her.

As I signed the guest ledger in a lobby whose opulence verged on vulgarity I asked the clerk where I could securely store a wagon loaded with photographic equipment and chemicals. He sniffed before each sentence he spoke, as though an air of imperiousness might counteract his hickish demeanor.

"You can store it where you stable your animal, sir," he said. "Burwick's livery is across the street and they'll lock it away real tight for you."

"Pardon me, sir," said a small, portly man standing nearby as I walked away from the desk holding the room key. He wore a well-cut suit of gabardine, and he spoke so quietly that it was necessary to lean in closely to understand what he was saying. This, I surmised, was due to embarrassment over his pronounced lisp.

"I don't mean to eavesdrop, but am I to understand that I am addressing a member of the photographic profession?"

"You are," I said.

"My name is Daniel B. Silas. I am an attorney-at-law, and it happens that I have a client who's in need of a good photographer. You are staying only for the night, or could you be persuaded to stay in our city for a day or two?"

My head was cocked at quite an angle trying to understand him, and at first I heard "city" as "shitty," but I maintained my poise and didn't snicker. "Our plan was to depart in the morning," I said, trying to appear casually disinterested but in fact overjoyed at the prospect of recouping what this extravagant interlude was draining from our meager savings. “I would have assumed that a town of this size was full of photographic studios.”

“Yes, sir, it is.” He looked around the lobby as though afraid he’d be overheard saying something incriminating, which piqued my interest further. “None of them will take this job. On moral grounds.”

“Aha,” I said. “I understand. That’s not something I’d be willing to risk, either. In any event the world is already full of ‘girlie’ photographs.” I had no moral objections to dirty pictures, certainly—I had after all taken a few, purely for my own pleasure, back in Kansas—but I didn’t wish to run the risk of having them confiscated, thereby drawing attention to myself.

I had shocked him, and he hastened to correct my misapprehension. “Oh, no, sir, you mistake my intent. What this gentleman wants isn’t anything objectionable. His problem is the local fellows either think it’s buncombe or they can’t make it happen.”

“Can’t make what happen?”

He looked around, as though someone unseen might be listening, then leaned in just as I was doing.

“Make the spirits of the dead appear,” he whispered, his eyes widening for effect. “On a wet plate.”

Of course it was buncombe, of the purest and most foolish kind, but if there was money in it, I was hardly in a position to turn it down. I’d never made a spirit photograph before but the gist of it was simple double exposure, and the examples I'd seen of the genre seemed either inartistic or unconvincing or both, and I loved a challenge.

"Oh, I can make them appear. Tell me, who's this gentleman?"

THAT NIGHT MAGGIE and I ate in the hotel dining room, she dressed in the one fine gown that remained to her and the only jewels she hadn't sold during our flight from Kansas and I wearing my least shabby suit. I looked perfectly unworthy of her company and was aware that the waiter's eyebrow was raised in condescension aimed at only me.

Maggie appeared completely unaware of it, however, and lapped at her lobster bisque and dissected her roast pheasant as calmly as if she still ate that way every night. She radiated a great relief, however, at this temporary restoration of her social station, and I brought up the possibility that we might spend another night there.

"That would be lovely, Bill," she said, seemingly unconcerned about the cost, and then the headwaiter brought over the *carte des desserts*, at which point we dismissed the topic.

THAT NIGHT, AS I lay abed staring at the finely wrought plasterwork on the ceiling, all my physical wants having been satisfied, Maggie spoke to me in a measured tone I had heard her use with her husband, on those occasions where she wanted it to appear that she was merely making a suggestion, whereas in fact she was making a nonnegotiable demand.

"It's awfully nice to lie in a proper bed, Bill." Here I knew I was due for trouble, for she'd pointedly never complained about the hardships of a mostly outdoor existence, and I'd known for weeks that she longed to furnish me with a litany of grievances, legitimate ones in her case, for she was a city girl and a fancy one at that. "Don't think it hasn't been a fine adventure, parts of it, anyway. Until June I'd never spent a night of my life under the stars, and it was lovely for a while, but I'll drown myself before I'll spend the winter in a tent."

"Naturally when winter comes we'll go south where it's temperate."

"I won't. I want to go to Greeley and rent a house."

I winced a bit at the mention of the name. She had read about the Greeley Colony in the Colorado Territory, a utopian community whose aims appealed mightily to her; I found them inane and impractical. Maggie was, however, a woman of varied, eccentric, and passionate enthusiasms, spiritualism having briefly been one of those, and as these had a way of passing quickly I had hoped she'd abandon the idea of settling in Greeley. It did occur to me now that it was likely filled with the sort of people who might pay money for photographs of the spectral representations of their departed dear ones.

"We don't know if they have need of a photographer," I said, not bothering to mention my other erstwhile occupation, saloonkeep, since such a job was nonexistent in teetotal Greeley.

"It doesn't matter, Bill, they'll find something for you. You've farmed before."

Not for long, I hadn't. I loathed farming more than I'd hated being in the army. But she was right; we had to land somewhere eventually, and she wasn't made for the rough life of a transient peddler. "All right," I said, "we'll head down there as soon as we quit Omaha."

THE NEXT DAY, shortly before midday, I set out for the estate of Colonel Joshua Cudahy with the photographic wagon, pulled by my very tired, very old, uncomplaining paint, Brutus. Every mile or so he'd utter a grunt and drop a road apple, and for the time of year it was not an unpleasant ride.

Shortly after midday I arrived. The estate was near Bellevue, some nine miles to the south of the city, the house at its center designed in the geographically inappropriate manner of a neoclassical antebellum plantation house. Its exterior, at least, had fallen into considerable disrepair. Upon several loud administrations of the door knocker—iron, and in the shape of a lion's head—I was greeted at the door by a silent, elderly butler wearing a frayed morning coat and an expression of deep puzzlement. Handing him my card I told him I was expected, and he disappeared into the house without speaking, shutting the door in my face.

There was no other habitation within a mile in any direction. The grounds were sumptuously wooded, and I thought it would be a good spot to put up a new house, though the one that stood now was an eyesore. I didn't guess it to be more than thirty or forty years old, but the aura of irreversible decay that clung to it gave it the feel of a much older ruin. The boards of the roof of the porch needed whitewashing, the windows were dirty and in several cases cracked, and the oaken Corinthian columns were cracked vertically on the concave portions of its striations and doubtless ready to collapse; still, this had plainly once been an opulent place. I saw the smoldering ruins of such a house in Georgia at the end of the war.

I understood Colonel Cudahy to have been a fur trader with some past association with Mr. John Jacob Astor, and it surprised me that no local photographer had both the skills and low moral character necessary to cheat so rich a man. Whether the current condition of the premises was due to an old man's neglectfulness or to a reduction in station, he had plainly been at one time a man of considerable means.

The butler reappeared and gestured for me to enter, again without speech, and I entered a vast, gloomy foyer in which stood a grizzly, rising up on its hind legs, mouth agape, forelegs poised to swat the viewer into the next world. Like the house and butler the bear was rapidly rotting, claws splintering, one glass eye gone altogether and the other cloudy, fur worn to bare, leathery skin in patches, the taxidermist's understructure showing in others.

"I shot her myself in '42, on the Platte. Would have finished me had I misfired. Left her cubs on the side of the river to die. Felt a little sorry for that later."

The voice startled me, coming from behind, high in pitch and rustic in tone, and with the considerable volume customary with the newly hard of hearing. I spun on my heels to find myself addressing a man who almost looked capable of felling such a beast barehanded. Dressed in a badly worn-down buckskin suit, he had quite a splendid head of silver hair that he wore swept back and down to the shoulder, and even slightly stooped as he was he must have topped six feet three inches. His eyes, black and staring intently from beneath a pair of bushily simian brows, called to mind Brady's photograph of John C. Calhoun, perhaps the most frightening-looking statesman America has yet produced.

"I'm Bill Sadlaw," I said, holding out my right hand, which he ignored. I hadn't gotten used to the name yet, and I still felt every time I said it that I'd be caught out as a liar, but Cudahy took right to it.

"Sadlaw. I knew a Sadlaw in Canada, about '26, '27. Cheated his partner out of about a hundred pounds' worth of beaver pelt, sold it to some Iroquois who moved it along to the French. Partner, name of Harlick, sawed off this Sadlaw's head, stuck it on a pole outside their camp as a warning. The one time I saw it it was pretty rotten, just a skull with hair sticking to it, and I asked Harlick what he was warning of. 'Tom Harlick's sawblade,' was his answer. Don't suppose that's any kin of yours."

"No, sir," I said. "I don't believe any of us ever made that far north."

"Well, sir, Dan Silas come by this morning and told me you could conjure a phantom onto glass. Is that so?"

"I have done," I said, "but I'm curious as to why you don't have a local man do it."

"Three told me it was chicanery. A fourth tried to prove them right by stealing a tintype of my Letitia and placing a copy onto the background of a picture of me. Don't know how it was done but it were such a patent fake I beat him within an inch of his death and wrecked his studio, smashed his camera and lenses and whatnot, and then saw to it that he made his way out of the state of Nebraska."

I nodded in a sage manner, only slightly more trepidatious about my plan to try and fool the old goat. "Rightly so," I said.

"Then there were three others who made attempts but captured nothing."

"Have you attempted a medium?"

He laughed, and it sounded like a three-hundred-pound hog snorting over its dinner. "Table knockers and seers! Buncombe. I want photographic proof." He lowered his voice. "I hear her, you see? All the time. And her gone fifteen years now. But I can't prove it's her, can't prove I'm not bereft of my reason."

"She speaks to you?" His own tentative autodiagnosis of *non compos mentis* seemed a plausible one to me.

"Whispers. And I hear doors closing, drawers being opened."

I found myself shouting at him just to match his considerable volume, and I wondered how whispering Dan Silas made himself understood to his client. "Your butler? Does he hear her too?"

"He's deaf as a plank," the Colonel shouted, waving his hand across his face, and I wondered if the bellowing wasn't out of sheer habit.

There was an element of risk in this, certainly, but I felt sure that the previous fraudster had been undone by a lack of artistry and technical finesse. "Now, Colonel, I should tell you that I'm currently working with a stereoscopic camera."

"I've nothing against it. Hell, seems to me that would make it well-nigh impossible for you to falsify such a thing."

That wasn't the case at all but I nodded my agreement. "I don't see how one could."

I HIED TO the wagon, fed Brutus a lump of sugar from my hand, and took down my tripod and the case containing the camera. Once I had them in the house I returned to fetch my plates and chemicals, and by the time I had coated the plates with collodion the Colonel had already changed into a black wool suit and cravat twenty years out of fashion. "Was this a suit you owned when Mrs. Cudahy was still living?" I asked in a moment of inspiration.

He looked down at it as if to remind himself of which suit he'd just donned. "Seems to me it was," he said.

"Good, that often helps, having objects familiar to the deceased," I said, thinking myself clever for inventing spiritualist lore on the spot.

I set him up in the brightest room on the first floor, the parlor, which featured a large picture window with a thin white curtain that diffused the daylight nicely. He was seated in a chair upholstered in crushed green velour, the least worn piece of furniture I'd seen so far, and he had such an air of dignified antiquity that I felt a certain revulsion at the fact that I was cheating him. Then I reminded myself, as any number of other phony spiritualists must have done, that I was comforting him with proof that his wife's love for him had survived death.

"Will you return tomorrow with the finished pictures?" he asked when the sitting was finished.

"I will, regardless of the outcome. You do understand we may be disappointed by the results," I said, hoping that I wouldn't lose my nerve, and also that my skills would prove equal to the task at hand.

He handed me a fifty-cent piece, at which I raised an eyebrow, hoping that he didn't think that my fee would be so cheap, but I'd misunderstood. "Come 'round about sunset. And when ye return, do me a favor and bring me back two pounds of salt, ground, would ye?"

"Certainly," I said, perfectly incurious as to his motive, and took my leave.

I HASTENED IN the wagon back to Omaha, though all the chemicals and equipment necessary for developing and printing the plates were in my wagon. It was well that the old bird hadn't had his picture made since the days of tintypes, because if I'd had to show him the results as they were I'd have had to declare failure. The greater part of my labors would be performed in Omaha, at the hotel.

THE STEREO VIEWS came out nicely, though not so nicely that I didn't regret the loss of the trusty old camera I'd had to leave behind in Cottonwood when we went on the run. There were four of them, and I thought one should be unaltered for appearance's sake; I chose for this the best of the views, and then I created a second negative of an amorphous haze using a lantern behind a sheet of muslin. This, superimposed onto the second plate, created the illusion of a partially materialized spectral body, roughly where the heart of a person standing next to the Colonel's chair would have been. Seen through the stereopticon it was quite convincing and gave me a slight chill when I first saw a finished composite print. For the third plate I did something similar, with the luminous entity somewhat larger. And for the last one I made one more of the glowing, shapeless blob, after which I took several negatives of Maggie's lovely, delicate hands at a distance from the lens that matched as closely as possible the Colonel's, at roughly the level of his shoulders. It took me a while on the hotel roof to get the perfect print of the fourth view (the first three were so nearly effortless I wondered whether I shouldn't make a profession of this), but when I had it, it was a thing of beauty, indisputably one of the most artistic images I'd ever made.

Colonel Joshua Cudahy, in the winter of his years, sat weary in a fine oaken chair, and at his side floated a filmy apparition that might have been human in form or not, but for the proof offered by her hands, sufficiently materialized to register as they rested, transparent but unmistakably those of a woman, on the Colonel's shoulders, as though the right arm were spanning his back and the left crooked to caress. The expression of weariness in his old eyes, the delicate interplay of light and shadow, the matching of negative to negative—they were all perfect, and perfection is an end I always attempt but seldom achieve.

MAGGIE CONCURRED, AND she had no qualms about fooling the old fellow. She said that the notion that Cudahy thought that he was being haunted by the woman he'd loved was like something out of Sir Walter Scott (whom I doubt she'd ever read), and she was certain that if he sensed it, then it must be true. The fact that I was concocting sham pictures to convince him of the same did nothing to discourage her rapt interest in the enterprise, and in fact it was difficult to convince her that she couldn't come along with me to present them to him. But if he understood that I had a female confederate, it might lead him to question whether those hands on his shoulders were those of his late wife's otherworldly manifestation, and so I promised to relay to her a full accounting of his reaction.

THAT NIGHT WE ate a much more modest supper, to my relief and at Maggie's own suggestion, at a small restaurant operated by a German couple who laughed at my accent but complimented my fluency, telling me I spoke good German "*für ein Ausländer.*" The thick white sausages accompanied with sweet mustard and sauerkraut and a bottle of Rhine wine that we consumed pleased me considerably more than the previous night's princely meal, and I felt a great sense of peace and satisfaction that I had succeeded in heading off my putative wife's impending rage.

As Maggie prepared to sleep I found myself restless. I put my clothes back on and left the hotel, wandering the streets until I found a saloon that looked hospitable instead of murderous, its patrons smoking cigars and laughing but not shouting at one another in a way that promised violence. Another point in its favor was that there were no women present, for in Omaha the only females in bars were there to provide services for which I had no more need that night.

The bartender brought me my shot of rye and my draught of lager and I dropped the Colonel's half-dollar onto the bar. There was a poker machine at the far end, and though I rarely found such devices tempting I dropped a nickel of my change into the slot and cranked the handle back. The machine dealt me three eights, upon which it deposited four nickels into the oval receptacle at the bottom of its cast-iron body. This was when I became aware of the presence of a tall and very drunken sot at my elbow.

"Three eights. You know what that signifies?" He had long, oily black hair that hung in strings past his shoulders, and a long, well-trimmed beard, and he stared intently at me with tiny dark eyes, set a little too close together.

"I do not."

"Three eights is twenty-four. Which is my age at the present time."

"That's remarkable," I said, trying hard to keep any tone of amusement out of my voice, since drunks who sense that they are being patronized can erupt in unexpected ways. And it was remarkable, because I would have guessed him to be forty at the very least; if he was telling the truth, then he must have led a dissolute life indeed.

"There is an art and a science to interpreting coincidence, sir."

"Oh."

"Of course what the average man calls coincidence is in fact no such thing at all. Are you familiar with your Holy Bible?"

"Intimately," I said, neglecting to add that I didn't lend it much credence.

"For the price of a drink I would be happy to explain to you how various signs and wonders can be used to explain the world and its sundry denizens, and help us navigate the treacherous moral waters that surround us."

"The price of a drink?"

"Not every Christian is a temperance man, sir. Jesus, after all, turned water into wine."

In the light of the gas lamp he swayed so hard he had to keep a hand on the bar to keep from toppling, and though his voice was firm I surmised he'd sampled a good bit of the stuff that very evening, just as I imagined the water-into-wine line was one he delivered two or three times a night. Nonetheless I felt magnanimous and fortunate in having been given, and satisfactorily completed, a difficult and remunerative task; so I bought him his drink and listened to his notions regarding using the Bible to tell the future. It involved numerology, by virtue of converting Greek letters (to my surprise he did display an admirable knowledge of the language) into integers, the whole enterprise vividly suggestive of madness.

"How did you come to conceive these theories of prophecy?" I asked him.

"I was born covered in a caul, and you know what that means to the ignorant. And so I was always being asked as a child to divine the future, which of course I had no earthly way of doing. And as the years went by I became interested in the notion that the Bible holds all the prophecy the world could want, if only we had the means to decipher its secrets. And so I began to study the book, but before long I realized that the true Bible was in Greek, not English or Latin. And there was in my hometown a very learned man, who volunteered to teach me Greek, and do you know that once I'd mastered the language I predicted the death of my tutor? And not a week later he was beaten to death by his own brother in a fight over a parcel of land. And I knew then that I had cracked it. And if you'll advance me the price of another drink, I'll gladly predict what's to come for you."

I can't say what caused me to turn down his offer; I certainly didn't believe a bit of it, but there was something unclean about the fellow and I didn't want him messing with my future one way or the other. I did buy him another libation, and left.

AT FOUR THE next afternoon I took the wagon back to Bellevue, Brutus pulling at a pace more deliberate than was his habit. He was too old for this sort of labor, but I couldn't afford a new horse any more than I could countenance the notion of condemning him to the glue factory, so I made allowances for his debility and resigned myself to longer travel times.

The day was cold but the sky was blue and the light clear, rendering the landscape's colors exceptionally vivid; the few clouds above me were perfectly white toward the top, fading to pale blue and orchid in their shadows beneath. Not for the first time I wished I could have been a painter instead of a photographer, if only for the possibility of preserving those fleeting colors for posterity.

Several miles outside Bellevue I again reached the Cudahy mansion, where the butler let me in and led me to the parlor to await the master of the house. There I found Mr. Daniel B. Silas waiting also, and we quickly ran out of conversational pleasantries and sat clearing our throats, an awkward interlude that gave me the opportunity to examine a pair of old paintings hanging on the wall, both of which appeared in the photographs. They were brown and nearly opaque with a too-heavy coat of varnish, but it was no less clear that each had been made by the same hand, and that the painter had had little or no training. Still there was something pleasing about them, elk standing awkwardly around a watering hole with mountains in the distance in the first (one of the elk had an extra limb), and a bear much like the one in the entryway in the second. There was a demented rage in the bear's eyes that was to my liking; it had been painted without much skill but with a passion.

When Cudahy finally descended he was in a scowling, silent temper that was hard to decipher; was it melancholy or rancor or fear of the spirit world that kept him so quiet? He was wearing his buckskin suit again, and he seemed even older than he had the previous afternoon. By this time the last light was gone from the sky, and the butler limped into the parlor with a brightly glowing oil lamp. I produced a handheld Holmes stereograph and extended the first of the views.

"Nothing," he said, sounding neither pleased nor displeased, though quite as loud as ever, and handed it to Silas, who stuck out his lower lip and squinted.

"Well, perhaps. Is that something there in the corner?" he said, proving that the mind is always prone to tricking itself, since this was the lone unadulterated view.

"Might be, I didn't see much in that one," I said, taking the contraption back and reloading it with the second card. Cudahy took it from me and peered through the lenses with a scowl.

"That some sort of fog, by your reckoning, or a fault in the picture?" he asked.

"I asked myself that same question at first sight. A leaky bellows will produce a similar effect, and the same thing shows up in the third view."

Now Silas looked, wheezing slightly as he did so. "Might could be something there, Colonel."

I loaded the third view and Colonel Cudahy grunted. "More mist," he said, turning it over to Silas and appearing to lose interest. "Don't imagine that's proof one way or the other, might be her or it might be you need a new apparatus."

I took the viewer back from Silas before he was quite ready to surrender it and loaded the fourth view. "That was what I was thinking to myself until I saw this one beginning to emerge in the printing frame."

Cudahy took it as though it were a loaded pistol. "Do ye mean to tell me you've captured proof of her existence on this here piece of cardboard?"

"I don't know about proof. I've seen such pictures before, but never one that made me shudder so."

Behind his moustache Silas looked perfectly spooked, and the color had drained right out of his face. "Have a look, Colonel," he said, and the tone of his whisper had gone up a good octave.

Cudahy placed the eyepiece of the viewer to his forehead, and for a moment all three of us stopped breathing; in my case, out of fear that he would see through my fakery, in Silas's from a terror of the undead, and in the Colonel's case I was left to wonder, until he flung the stereoscope away from him like a cottonmouth and pulled his chair back from the table. "Goddamn," he howled.

Naturally, I assumed the worst. Would I be sent to jail? Could I be prosecuted for creating a bogus spirit picture? Was there any law against such a forgery?

Silas being too frightened to retrieve the viewer, I walked over to where it lay, biding my time in an attempt to come up with an excuse. But I was wrong; Cudahy believed.

"She's been here all along! And now I've proof! And proof that she means to do me in!" His voice had begun taking on a more rustic quality, as though his excitement were burning away a layer of acquired civilization.

"Do you in?"

"Damn it, man, you seen her hands around my throat!"

"Begging your indulgence, Colonel, but it seems to me those hands are placed affectionately at your shoulders," I said.

"You didn't know her! She means to see me dead before my time and I won't have it. Did ye bring the salt?"

"I did, Colonel. I left it on your porch."

"Haul it in, then. We'll rid this house of that creature from hell one way or another and I'll live out my years in peace!"

I went out to the porch, equal parts relieved that he hadn't caught me out and puzzled as to his intentions for the salt. There were two bags full and I dropped them onto the table in the parlor.

"Good. I'll start clockways out the front door, you start t'otherways and we'll meet halfway. Between us we'll have it done before she knows what came at her!"

"Again, sir, begging your patience, I'm unclear as to your aim."

"Oh," he said. "I understand, you'll be wanting your pay.

I don't begrudge you a penny of it, my lad." At that he reached into his pocket and pulled out a small gunnysack sewn shut with twine and tossed it at me, coins clinking inside. I had not ever named a price, hoping that his surprise at my results would make him carelessly generous. Desperate though I was to know the amount he'd handed me, I didn't wish to appear greedy and so pocketed the bag without opening it, and the desire to know what further work was required of me compelled me to ask him what was to be done with the salt.

"Surround the perimeter. She won't be able to cross a line of salt, will she?" He was giddy now, laughing in an even louder voice than he'd been using, and he headed for the front door. "Pay particular care to the doors and windows."

I looked over at Silas, who was now staring into the stereopticon, presumably at the fourth view, for his lower lip was now visible and trembling.

"Did you know he was mad when you engaged me?" I asked.

"He's not mad, look at the picture, damn you!" Finally Silas's voice was raised to a normal volume. "You'd best secure the perimeter as he told you to do, I'd not want to be around him when he's been disobeyed."

Outside I started counterclockwise, pouring a line of salt around the walls, executing a double layer at the windowsills and the side door that led to the kitchen, where through the window I spied the butler sitting quietly at a table, and he watched me pouring the salt with a notable lack of curiosity.

Around the back of the house I met up again with Colonel Cudahy, his face deeply flushed and his breathing heavy, a grin of sinister elation on his lips. "We've got her trapped, son. Go tell Silas and Jacques-Louis to come on out of there."

"Silas and who?"

"My majordomo, you'll have to guide him by the elbow, he doesn't hear anything."

I wanted more than anything else to be away from him, and so I returned to the house and informed Mr. Silas that his presence was required on the front lawn. He was still staring at the last of the stereo views. "I've never known such a woman's love, that she'd return from the grave just to torment me," he said as he stood and shambled toward the front door. "To think that he doesn't want such a thing."

I caught up with the ancient butler, who was still at the table, dozing now, head cupped in his palm. I pointed at the front door and he nodded, rose with a terrific groan, and began to walk painfully out of the kitchen.

Once we were assembled on the carriageway before the house the Colonel began a long tirade that dealt with, among other subjects, vengeful spirits, his opinion of the reputation of President Andrew Jackson (inflated, in Cudahy's view), the importance of stressing arithmetic over reading in the education of young children, the barbarity of the German tongue, the inadvisability of eating mollusks no matter what the month, and, finally, the natural tendency of women to want to murder the men with whom they cohabit.

"It's because of what we do to their nether parts they hate us, and I don't rightly blame them. As a lad amongst the fur traders in Canada I had to submit to such indecencies and once I was big enough to do so I kilt several who treated me as I treated my wife. Although she never complained and even affected to like it when I placed my wacker in her hot place! Her lies made me aware that she detested the sight of me and when she passed I knowed she was going to stay about the house, just waiting for her chance to do me in! But now I've proved her presence and it's time for a reckoning. She's trapped in there and she will be destroyed! Not a trace shall remain on this earth and she by God will have moved on as is proper, either to heaven or hell as the Lord God wills it but her stay on earth will be done!"

He was so worked up it was difficult to get him to hear me when I attempted to interrupt, but finally he heard me ask my question. "How do you mean to destroy her, Colonel?" I asked this partly out of actual curiosity as to how his brain had concocted such a plan and partly out of real concern for the physical well-being of all present.

"By God, man, they's only one way to get rid of a haint! And that's a blaze. Nothing cleanses like a good fire!" And with that he ran inside the house.

There was quite a bit of noise as Silas, the butler, and I watched the house, uncertain and afraid. I had no desire to enter the house and do battle with even a superannuated man of Cudahy's size and mental state, and my companions seemed more puzzled than afraid. There was a loud crash, followed by a burst of flames through the parlor windows, and then another crash, which I now understood to be the dumping of a barrel of something flammable, followed by flames coming through the kitchen window. Now fire was also visible through the front door, having made its way into the foyer, and I thought I glimpsed the Colonel bounding up the central staircase. I could certainly hear him laughing with the gleefulness of a small child watching a pony trick at the circus, and I asked Silas if he had known Cudahy to be suicidal in the past.

"The Colonel?" he said in a tone of great offense. "Such a man, a self-murderer? Take it back, sir!"

Now the upstairs was ablaze, sour black smoke roiling from all the downstairs windows. Cudahy could now be heard singing "Camptown Races" as he moved from chamber to chamber, setting alight the amassed detritus of a lifetime. Then he appeared in a window, silhouetted by orange firelight, dancing a sort of jig, his movements so happy that I couldn't see interrupting them or trying to block his joyfulness. And then I decided I couldn't watch him die, that I, in fact, was partially responsible for his state of mind. And so it was that I charged against my better judgment into the burning mansion of Colonel Joshua Cudahy with an eye toward dragging him out to safety.

"Are you mad?" cried Silas as I took the porch steps two at a time and burst through a curtain of flame that separated the stairway from the front door, and I took those steps two and even three at a time until I reached the second story, where I found fire barring my way to my left and my right. I heard the Colonel singing "Oh! Susanna" in remarkably poor voice in the latter direction, then took down from the window a wool curtain that hadn't yet started burning, wrapped it around myself, and pushed through the flames into a bedchamber where, illuminated by a fire that was rapidly consuming a bed ticked with straw, I saw the Colonel dancing with an empty dress and giggling between lyrics.

The smoke was thickening and made it hard to vocalize, but I managed to shout at him. "Colonel, you have to go or you'll burn," I said, but he seemed not to hear.

I tapped him on the shoulder. "Colonel!" I yelled.

"There'll be no cutting in here!" he shouted back at me. "This dance is mine!"

Though considerably aged he was a good deal larger than me, and clearly bereft of his reason, and so bearing in mind the supposed strength of the mad I slugged him as hard as I could in the belly. His uninhabited dress of a dance partner took much of the force out of the blow, however, and he swore at me with such ferocity that when he pulled back his fist to hit me I feared he'd knock me unconscious and doom me to roast by his side.

I was fortunate in that his aim was poor; I dodged the blow and decided to make one more effort before saving my own carcass. I picked up a small side table next to the burning bed and threw it at the window, shattering several of the panes and bringing in a draught of cold air that caused the flames within the room to swell larger and brighter. I battered the window frames with the table until there was room to get through, and I was so absorbed in this activity that it was only then I noticed the old man pulling at my sleeves.

"You're breaking my window, ye insolent cur!"

I reared back and swung at him with the little table, intending merely to get him out of my way so that I could jump; but in an attempt to avoid the blow he fell back against the window, at which point I gave him a good, solid shove, and he fell out of the window and onto a shrub beneath, a conifer of some kind. I guessed it had been planted there as an ornament, though neglect had allowed it to grow into an unattractive shape that nonetheless afforded Colonel Cudahy a relatively soft landing. Between the fire and the shrub his decision to put on his buckskins had been a fortuitous one.

I hastened to climb out the window myself and jumped, aiming to his right onto another shrub. Its perennial stem was quite solid and so were the multiple branches extending from it; my landing was painful, but I was alive, if coughing and hacking like a consumptive with a cheroot in his jaws. I pulled the Colonel up out of the other bush and helped him to his feet.

"You've got some balls on you, throwing me out my own

got-damn window!" His bellow was raspy and thick from the smoke, but they still must have heard him all the way back in Omaha.

Mr. Silas came stumbling toward us. "You're saved, sir, praise Jesus."

"Saved?" He turned and looked at the house. "Saved from that vengeful haint! You're right, Silas."

"Saved from the conflagration, Colonel."

His face a tawny orange in the reflection of the fire, it seemed to dawn on him that his arsonous handiwork might have done him in. "So I am."

He then sat his large frame down on the lawn and began sobbing. "I have sinned against you, Letitia," he said, over and over again.

BRUTUS WAS UNACCUSTOMED to pulling the wagon after nightfall, and whinnied in mild protest as I drove him back to Omaha, but the cool breeze of the night felt good on my face, which in the morning would be as red as if I'd spent a July day in the sun without a hat. Arriving in town I put him up at the stable and had the boy lock the wagon in for the night, and crossing the street to the hotel I realized that I still hadn't counted my money.

Entering the room I found Maggie asleep, and I lit the lamp and quietly opened the little gunnysack, from which I then extracted, to my great surprise, a brand-new double eagle, which nearly caused me to shout, not least because there were more coins inside, along with some dried juniper leaves and various other conjurer's herbs. Ten double eagles were stacked on the writing desk that overlooked the street downstairs, which at this hour was reasonably quiet, with just a single pair of drunks arguing over a bottle of laudanum below, and listening to the muffled sounds of their murderous threats I sat marveling at my good fortune in encountering Colonel Cudahy. I had two hundred dollars in gold, enough to buy a share in the Greeley Colony with some left over. Notions of fate and destiny are for the weak-minded and superstitious and frequently lead such men into disaster; still, it seemed to me that night as though such forces were drawing me to the Colorado Territory, and for the first time in months I felt lucky.

FOUR YEARS LATER

ONE

Denver, Colorado, March 1878

The Wm. O. Sadlaw Photographic Studio and Gallery

With the eastern range of the Rocky Mountains in the near distance and the smell of creosote and horseshit mingling in my nostrils I sat on the flat rooftop, exposing prints and idly contemplating the great rectangles of glass that comprised the skylight of my studio. This was one of those rare occasions when my lost Maggie's face surfaced unbidden in my mind's eye, inspiring the slightest twinge of regret; the steel-sharp print slowly emerging before me of a scowling, bejeweled bulldog of a Denver matron seemed a rebuke to the memory of that evanescent visage. The day was bright and the temperature mild, and the mountains in the short distance looked close enough for a stroll. Ostensibly I was engaged in the making of prints for sale, but the printing-out paper in the frames required only direct sunlight and no attention from me, and in fact I sat cross-legged on the tar paper and basked, thumbing through Aeschylus and wondering how quickly I could rush the afternoon's scheduled portrait sittings and be gone. Where I went didn't matter to me, only that I went.

I didn't look up as the hinges of the trapdoor announced the arrival of Lemuel, my housekeeper's yellow-haired idiot nephew. She didn't seem particularly to like him but had worked hard to make me hire him four months before when my previous helper set off for the mountains to prospect silver, and the boy's eager industriousness made up for his lack of intellect. His eyes were tiny and close-set, and his mouth generally open slightly, and even when it was closed his lower incisors and canines showed against his upper lip, giving him the outward aspect of a particularly dim terrier. I hoped he would see me reading and understand that I didn't want to answer his question, whatever it was.

"Mr. Sadlaw?" he said. "There's two ladies downstairs want to see you about something."

"Hell's bells," I said without looking up, concentration fractured. I stood and checked the progress of the prints in their frames, cursing. The boy cringed like a whipped pup at my quiet tirade, and I asked him what was the matter.

"Nothing, Mr. Sadlaw." His voice had changed but it occasionally still shifted into the higher registers, usually when I was annoyed with him.

"I ever hit you, boy?" He shook his head no. "Why the hell do you always act like I'm about to, then?" He shrugged and scurried down the trapdoor. Upon hiring him I had been struck by his ripe odor, considerable even by the standards of Denver at that time. It called to mind a wound whose dressing badly wanted changing, and after three days working in close quarters I added to his weekly duties a bath, to be taken at Hinshaw's Barber Shop down the street and put on my tab.

Following the wretch I found two women in the gallery, one of them examining the views in the box stereopticon, letting out little gasps at each new view. Like the studio, the gallery was skylit, and two rows of display counters ran along the walls. At the end of one, next to the stairway leading outside, was a piano, which the second woman had uncovered and on which she tinkled out an air I recognized as Chopin's, though I couldn't have named it. I noted with satisfaction their expensive dress and sauntered over to where the first one stood.

"Are you interested in arranging a sitting?" I asked, and she giggled.

"Not as yet," she said. "We were anxious to inquire about the price of such a sitting." She was tall and buxom, with an oddly fetching horsey quality and a tendency to overenunciate that seemed newly learned. At her bosom was a diamond brooch, and pearls dangled from her ears. Her petite friend at the piano was more conventionally pretty and less interested in having her picture taken, I thought. As the first of the two explained to me that any such expense would have to be approved by their husbands, the upright clock in the corner chimed two o'clock, time for my first sitters to arrive. The downstairs door opened and my customers mounted the stairs, as though they had been listening outside on the street for the chiming. I explained that I would have to be on my way and handed the lady a printed list of prices.

"Thank you, Mr. Sadlaw," she said, each syllable slightly too clipped. "I shall discuss the matter with my husband, Mr. Forsyth."

"I'll look forward to seeing you both soon, then." I bowed slightly and made my way with them to the entrance, where a stocky, bald-headed man stood next to a woman built like a broom, close to six feet tall and weighing, I would guess, no more than 120 pounds. They were both dressed for cold weather despite the warmth of the day, and I instructed the boy to begin the preparation of the plates.

When the couple had removed their outer garments they stood awkwardly, uncertain of where to stand or sit. She wore light gray silk with dark gray trimmings, as finely cut as could be had in Denver then, and despite her unusual frame looked quite handsome in the soft light of the early afternoon.

The studio had one glass wall in addition to its glass ceiling, and a series of thick, moveable black curtains. I adjusted the draperies until I had an agreeable light, then I had her sit down on a bench. I placed him behind her and instructed him to place his hand affectionately on the lady's shoulder. She looked as though a large pink spider had crawled there, and he as though he were fondling a cadaver. As I focused I tried to lighten the mood with a joke or two, but the upside-down image on the ground glass didn't get any happier.

"What's the occasion," I asked, thinking that a discussion might relax them a little. Instead his scowl intensified, and she turned away as though anxious to avoid provoking him further.

"We just want a goddamned picture to remember each other by," the man said. "You hurry up and take it."

At that moment Lemuel returned with the loaded plate holders; I ordered the boy upstairs to check the progress of the prints, smiled my most conciliatory smile at the curmudgeonly old bastard, and began taking pictures.

After the dyspeptic couple had gone and I had developed the plates, I prepared those for the next sitting and emerged from the darkroom. I was confronted then with a second couple, spooning like a pair of sixteen-year-olds on the upholstered bench opposite the piano, and it seemed a shame that the woman playing it hadn't stayed behind to serenade them. As young Lemuel was engaged on the roof and they hadn't seemed to notice me, I sat before the already exposed keyboard and gently began to coax “Beautiful Dreamer” from it. After a few bars I glanced over my shoulder and found them sitting bolt upright and embarrassed.

“Ready for your sitting?” I asked, and they both nodded. Despite their adolescent comportment they appeared to be in their thirties, the woman pretty and round-faced with corn silk hair and green eyes, the man heavy about the jaw, with wavy black hair and muttonchops. He wore a patch of white silk over his left eye, and when I moved them back into the studio he sat down and took it off. He seemed quite at ease as he extracted a box from his vest pocket and opened it to reveal an eye of glass. He stuffed the thing into its socket with a liquid pop while his wife, with no sign of squeamishness, tended to her hair. When their grooming was finished I arranged them together on a bench and asked them their preferences regarding pose and mood. He shrugged and she looked blank, and I suggested they move in closer to one another and look into one another’s eyes. When I had shot two of those I had them look straight at the camera, and then I amended the suggestion.

“Mr. Gill, why don’t you look over at her as she faces the camera?” It was less an aesthetic suggestion than a means to avoid wasting a negative on a grotesque pose that would result in no print orders. He understood my intentions better than I thought.

“Mr. Sadlaw, I don’t care a damn who sees I’ve got a marble eye.”

His wife nodded her enthusiastic assent. “I want to see his whole pretty face, if you don’t mind.” I shot the picture as requested, satisfied that I would sell it, and a few more besides that I wouldn’t have chanced without his blessing.

Finishing the plates in the darkroom afterward I found my thoughts wandering, for the first time in a very long while, in the direction of my old one-eyed friend Herbert Braunschweig of Cottonwood, Kansas. Over the years I had noted the town’s continuing presence on railroad maps as a stop on the milk run and nothing more; what had happened to any of its inhabitants after May of 1873 I couldn’t have said, nor whether I entered their thoughts at all, except as the killer of the town’s foremost citizen and, by extension, of its aspirations to greatness.

My third sitter of the afternoon failed to show up on time, and after half an hour’s wait I elected to leave. “What’ll I tell him if he shows up wanting his photograph made?” the boy asked.

“Tell him to take the sitting fee and invest in a goddamned timepiece,” I grumbled, straightening my necktie and preparing to leave. The boy was unsure whether to take me literally or not, and I clapped a friendly hand on his shoulder. “Or tell him I was called away by an emergency.”

The only emergency lay in the fact that the lady in question lived in Golden, ten miles away, and refused on principle to receive any unannounced suitor after the hour of five in the afternoon.

My housekeeper was just returning from the Chinese laundryman's with the day's clean load when I met her on the stairs, and made no response when I told her I wouldn't be home for dinner. A widow of fifty-five winters, hard ones by the look of her, she didn't approve of my courting habits, though she knew no details. She was round as a medicine ball, and in the course of her daily labors she regularly worked herself up into wheezing fits the sound of which terrified me; she assured me that they were nothing extraordinary and continued to work harder than any woman or man I ever saw.

Immediately upon arriving in Denver I'd advertised for a housekeeper; it had been years since I lived alone, and I knew I would require daily help in the running of the household if I were to get any work done. I was specifically looking for a woman of the least enticing physical type, with the hope of avoiding temptations that might lead to distracting complications, and Ralph Banbury, the editor of the *Denver Bulletin* and the owner of my building, had recommended Mrs. Fenster. She had worked in his house for some months before Mrs. Banbury decided she would be happier without her scowling presence and replaced her with a young Bavarian girl, whom Banbury bedded within the week.

Much later, in his cups, he admitted that if Mrs. Fenster's brother-in-law hadn't been one of the *Bulletin*'s pressmen, he would have joined the chorus of the town's other papers in calling for her arrest upon the death of Mr. Fenster, ten years previous. Her story was that she had returned from a visit to her sister in Georgetown to find her husband shot to death in their bed, but the opinion of the U.S. Marshal was that she had come home and found him alive and well and *in flagrante delicto* with the lonely wife of the greengrocer downstairs. Her refusal to pantomime either shock or grief did little to help her case in the public's mind, but neither the press nor the police ever succeeded in getting a word out of the other lady, who according to Banbury was so terrified of Mrs. Fenster that she left her husband and the state of Colorado six months later, never to return. Eventually the matter faded away without Mrs. Fenster ever having to spend a night away from her own blood-soaked bed, and a decade later the incident was largely forgotten.

Mrs. Fenster received three dollars a day from me six days a week (exactly twice what her sister's boy collected), and on Saturdays she went off into the night with another sister who was even fatter and more dyspeptic than she was, returning Sunday evenings subdued and moodier than usual. I had no idea what they got up to apart from the suspicion that it involved church; every Saturday night before leaving she laid my good black suit out, and every Sunday she returned to find it still laid out, unworn.

I MADE MY way to the roof and then down via the ladder to the courtyard below, the quickest way to the livery stable on the street behind mine. The studio and gallery were previously operated by a melancholy Prussian by the name of Ernst Nielander who, after three quarters of a decade of operation in Denver, documenting the layers of its social sediment from the opium fiends and harlots at the bottom to the silver tycoons at the top, had found himself yearning to practice his craft in his suddenly peaceable native land. His desire to return was so strong that I was able to purchase the business as a going concern for less than it was worth; when he returned a year later, disillusioned and disappointed, and wanted to buy it back for the same price, I laughed in his face. He left Denver again and, so far as I know, was never heard from thereafter.

Though the building was nearly perfect for the purpose it generally served, several eccentricities of design made it a less than ideal place to live. Among these was an outdoor johnny that could be accessed only by a ladder from the rooftop, for no access to the rear courtyard was provided from the interior of the building. The arrangement's only advantage was that it allowed me to exit the property via a gate behind the outhouse into an alley that ran between my property and the livery stable, though reentry via the gate was impossible.

It was nearly three when I drove my carriage out the door of the stable, bearing a bottle of nerve tonic, in case milady was still mad at me from last time, and foolishly dressed for the warmth of a spring day. When I reached Golden at 4:20 I was sorry for that, as there was still snow on the ground at that elevation, and the air on the drive up had chilled my face to what I imagined was a deep, salmon pink. I drove to a neat, two-story brick building among a row of similar structures, climbed down, and tied my animal to the post outside it, ignoring the clucking of a pair of passing women as they looked back and forth between me and the house with equal measures of disapproval. One of them muttered something that sounded like "harlot," and I turned to face them directly. In my hand I held a garland of bluebonnets I'd stopped to collect on the way up; I separated two blooms and brazenly proffered them to the horrified ladies, treating them to my most disarming and ingenuous smile.

"*Bel après-midi, n'est-ce pas, mesdames?*" I said, and they hurried on their way, sputtering at the vile and dissolute ways of the heathen French. I strode to the door, lifted the upcurled trunk of its brass elephant knocker, and dropped it to our rhythmic signal: one, two, three, then half a rest before four and five. Priscilla opened the door and looked me up and down with mild contempt. Dressed and coiffed with her habitual demure elegance, she looked as fresh-scrubbed and wholesome as a minister's wife on her way to teach a Sunday school class on chastity.

"I suppose you've come all the way from Denver looking for a piece of ass," she said.

I had no answer to that question. The truth wouldn't have been gallant and she would have seen through a lie, so I handed her the bluebonnets. She raised an eyebrow and frowned, but when I showed her the bottle of laudanum she moved aside to let me in.

Fifteen minutes later we were in her squeaking iron bed, hammering away at it like we'd only just met. She heightened my arousal with throaty cries that crescendoed and decrescendoed slowly, though whether expressing either real passion or a simple desire to gratify my *amour propre* only she knew. After such a long period of chastity the physical sensation of intercourse was nearly overwhelming, and shortly I discharged with a slightly piquant sensation what felt like a pint and a half of spunk. I resolved before withdrawal never to go that length of time again without a proper ejaculation. After we'd lain there for a while she spoke.

"You know I've been going to church, Bill?"

I sat up and took pains not to laugh. "You've seen the light?"

"Don't be smart. I just go to be sociable."

I thought about the biddies on the street and wondered what churchgoing ladies in Golden would welcome her in their homes. "Which church is that? The Methodist or the Baptist?"

"I take my carriage into Denver and go to the Presbyterian services and let it be known that I'm a widow. Last week some of the ladies invited me over to a tea."

"That's nice," I said.

"Well, for a bunch of ladies taking tea after church services the talk got pretty vile, I'll tell you that."

Now I did laugh. "How vile could it get?"

"I'm getting to that. One of the ladies was talking about a fellow from Denver who abandoned his wife for a banjo player."

"Beg pardon?"

"Well, this fellow apparently traveled the country as a sort of saltimbanque, he'd go into saloons and do a little tumbling, then he'd play his banjo and pass the hat."

"This is the fellow who left his wife?"

"No. The one who left his wife, left her for this banjo player here. Two gents, if you see what I'm getting at? So one of the ladies at tea manifested the same misunderstanding you did just now. But the more we explained it to her politely the more confused she got. And finally Mrs. Halliwell, the lady whose house it was, explained to her that the nature of the rapport between the two men was of . . . of love. Of a physical kind."

I nodded again.

"And the poor thing just wouldn't understand. I think there were several of them that didn't, quite, either, but this one kept asking and asking until finally Mrs. Halliwell broke down and explained that the one stuck his pecker in the other one's mouth."

I was thinking right then that I'd have given a thousand dollars to hear that Mrs. Halliwell explaining to her poor demure friend about cocksucking. "She said 'pecker'?" I asked.

"I think she said 'manhood.' Anyhow, having said it, Mrs. Halliwell brought up the fact that it's illegal, putting your mouth on someone else's reproductive parts."

"No, it's not," I said, though I knew it was most places, and probably here as well.

"Yes, it is. The law went after these two fellows and not just because the one deserted his wife." She took a deep breath and paused before expelling it. "Mrs. Halliwell, who was enjoying our ill ease, shocked the other ladies by saying there were women deviates who practice a form of the same vice. Pussy-licking. Well, if you don't think that got them all indignant. Most of them thought she was having us on. So it got me thinking."

"About me tonguing your pussy?"

She got red and looked off toward the doorway. "I don't know of anybody else who does that. I'd never even heard of it until you did it to me that first night."

"I thought you liked it," said I, knowing perfectly well she did.

"I do." She was quite flushed now. "But it's not natural, is it?"

"Sure it is."

"But it's not. Where did you learn it, anyway?"

"A lady whose husband wouldn't. He thought it was unnatural, too."

"Well. It's not that I don't enjoy it. But I feel so ashamed, just lying there and feeling lips and a tongue on it. Think of what else goes on down there."

I shrugged. "If you want me to quit it, I will."

"No," she said. "I've just been thinking, is all." She sat up, as though just remembering something. "And where exactly have you been all these weeks without a word?"

"In Denver, taking pictures. You could stop by and see the studio sometime if you wanted."

"I meant why've you not been by to see me?"

She sounded genuinely puzzled and a little wounded, and I wondered if she possibly could have forgotten the vicious tongue lashing she'd given me the last time I'd stopped by for a quick one. Among other things she'd expressed a wish never to see me again, a wish I'd promised to fulfill. I'd meant it, too, but I hadn't counted on the effect of weeks of celibacy on my stability and resolve, or on the contents of my scrotum. I'd had no desire to patronize the whores on Market Street, and the sin of Onan, which practice had been my sole sexual release for so many weeks, never provokes a sufficient volume of ejaculate to properly evacuate the nuts. (I remain convinced that the inevitable putrefaction of that residual semen is the cause of what we used to call in the army "blue balls.")

"You told me not to come back, ever," I said.

She slapped her hand down on my chest, playfully, but hard enough to hurt. "I was mad at you, you stupid man. That doesn't mean I truly didn't want you to come back," she said, in an absurdly coquettish tone for a naked woman speaking to a man who has recently had to extract one of her shortest and curliest poils from between his incisors.

I was about to dress and make my excuses, hoping to avoid another screaming fit, when a loud rapping came from the door downstairs: one, two, full rest, three four, full rest, five, six, and seven. Priscilla went rigid and sat straight upright, eyes wide and nostrils flared.

"What's the matter?" I asked her, and she hissed to quiet me down, then crept to the window on her knees. She lifted the corner of the curtain, then turned back to me in a panic.

"Isn't this Wednesday?" she asked.

"It's Thursday," I said, and she covered her mouth up with her hand. She kept shaking her head and crawled back to the bed. From outside came a cry, a man's voice. "Cilla!"

I went over to the window and peered through the edge of the lace curtain. Downstairs at the door stood my friend and landlord Banbury. He stood patiently and didn't act as though her failure to answer promptly was anything unusual. He consulted a pocket watch and continued to stand, facing the street.

"Well, for Christ's sakes, it's just Ralph," I said with some relief, tempered by a growing realization of the complexity of the situation facing me. "I thought he came over on Tuesdays and Fridays."

She shook her head. "Thursdays and Mondays, now."

"No use getting into a knot about it. I'll go let him in." I was already half dressed and buttoning my shirt.

"Are you crazy?" she said, trying to whisper but betrayed by her anger into half shouting.

"What else do you want to do? Turn him away? Have me stay here and listen from the wardrobe while you make the two-backed beast?" I moved toward the door and when I took the knob in hand the pitcher containing the bluebonnets shattered on the wall next to the jamb, dousing me with water.

"Son of a bitch!" That was said loud enough for Ralph to hear, at least the last, explosive word of it, and I made my way quickly down the stairs.

She was close behind me but she stopped cold when I opened the door. "Evening, Banbury," I said.

If he was surprised at the sight of me in his lover's doorway at the hour of their regular weekly assignation, he maintained his aplomb. "Sadlaw," he said, as nonchalant as if we had come across one another on the street.

"Come on in, I was just on my way. Cilla took today for Wednesday."

"I see. Perhaps I ought to come back another time."

"As I said, I was already on my way." Peering around me he saw her on the stairs, her dressing gown hurriedly wrapped about her shoulders and her feet accusingly bare, her auburn hair winding damningly down past her shoulders. His grin grew tighter and I shouldered my way past him with a faint apology. I heard her door closing and the sound of shouting, followed by those of a heavy object hitting a wall or the floor and glass breaking. Her curio cabinet, most likely, and certainly at her own hand; whichever of them had upended it, though, it would be Banbury who bought its replacement after the fighting had given way to tearful apologies, declarations of love, and finally to urgent copulation, likely as not right there on the downstairs canapé. I climbed aboard my buggy, sorry for their trouble but happy to be temporarily drained of the source of my own.

I STOPPED AT the dining room of the Wentworth House Hotel for a dinner of steak and fried potatoes, then made a visit to the Occidental Hall to have a glass of beer and see the miners and prospectors get themselves fleeced at the gaming tables. I watched one prospector in particular lose spin after spin on the roulette wheel, dropping a dollar or more on each try. His face was dotted with fresh scabs that suggested he'd tried to save money by shaving himself after a long abstinence, and he grew slightly more crestfallen with each successive failure of his luck to change. I watched the operator, too, and the cruel glimmer in his eye each time the wheel slowed and refused again to hand the wretch a small win, defying the laws of probability; fortunately for him the prospector's familiarity with mathematics was probably limited to the simplest arithmetic. After a while it stopped being funny, and I left the poor fellow to it and hoped he wouldn't lose his entire fortune trying to prove a point about luck.

TWO

The Origin of the World

The next morning was cold and overcast and useless for printing, and I went about my morning activities in an agitated state. This was made worse around midmorning when Augie Baxter turned up at the door with his sample case and an air of obsequious bonhomie that suggested bad news. I led him into my office and sat him down, and the boy brought us coffee in china cups.

"Sales are down," he acknowledged as I eyeballed my earnings. "Even atrocity pictures aren't moving like they used to do. I bet we didn't sell ten of your scalped buffalo hunter in the last six months."

According to my statement only seventy-three dollars and thirty-five cents were owing to me for the six months covered, less than what I still owed him for views of Paris and Rome and the land of the Hottentots I'd ordered on his last visit.

"I don't suppose I'll be making an order then, this time." I handed him the statement back.

"Wait." I turned back to find him rifling the sample case. "Let me show you something before you say that."

He handed me a single view, which I placed into the stereopticon. Pressing my eyes to the lenses I was treated to the sight of a naked woman leering at the camera, one hand demurely resting at her shoulder and the other stimulating her unusually hirsute genitalia. The look of wanton depravity on the woman's face and the artless explicitness of the pose set this view apart from the typical nude views sold in the back rooms of saloons and cigar stores and whorehouses, or, for that matter, from the ones I'd taken years before of Maggie. I was sad at the thought of those images I'd left behind in Cottonwood and apoplectic at the notion that someone might have found them, might at this moment be pulling them from a similar sample case somewhere for under-the-counter sale to slack-jawed, masturbating yokels unworthy of her glance.

"Not interested," I said.

"I was just showing you, is all." He took the view back and replaced it in the case's hidden compartment. "I sell a hell of a lot of these extra-dirty French views out of the cathouses, and if

I could get a few of some local gals who don't look like they're about to keel over from the last stages of the clap, in some real inviting poses, I could sell even more. I'd really like to start vending them under the counter in some of the finer galleries, like yours right here."

"Good luck," I said. "You won't be the first one who's tried."

Augie noticed the boy standing in the doorway before I did. "What do you want?" he asked with some belligerence.

Poor Lemuel cowered and shrank into the corridor, extending his hand to me. In it was an envelope. "Fellow just brought this by," he said. "Urgent message for you, Mr. Sadlaw."

He scurried out as I opened the envelope, which bore neither postage nor return address. Inside was a single sheet of stationery bearing the engraved flag of the *Denver Bulletin*, reduced to fit the page.

Sadlaw,
Meet me at the Charpiot Hotel at noon for luncheon.
R. Banbury

I shoved the envelope and the letter into my desk drawer. It was a quarter past eleven. "Sorry, Augie, I'm being summoned. You'll have to come back later."

"Fine, I'll head on down to Market Street and have a look at some of those whores." His eyebrows rose and fell dementedly, and he seemed to expect me to be impressed.

"You go and have yourself a good time," I said.

"I'll leave you these and come back for your order tomorrow."

I nodded as he pulled the samples and a catalogue from his case and set them on my desk, though I had no intention of making an order with so many sets of views unsold in the display cases.

AFTER INFORMING MRS. Fenster that I would not require any lunch, I descended to the street and strolled to my engagement at a leisurely pace, not particularly concerned about punctuality. The sky had remained low and dark gray, the day as cold as it had been at dawn, and I regretted not having put on a heavier coat. I arrived at the Charpiot shortly before noon and didn't see Banbury in the dining room. I told the maître d'hôtel whom I was meeting and was informed with a disdainful sniff that Mr. Banbury took his luncheon in his private suite of rooms on the third floor.

The corridors and the staircases of the Charpiot were finely wrought, with imported carpets and flocked velvet walls, and though I was dressed with more care than usual I still felt like the ashman misdirected through the parlor. I was certain that the staff and guests I passed on the way to the suite saw me the same way, and somehow certain also that Banbury had planned this humiliation as punishment for defiling his *inamorata*, though I knew this was absurd, since he'd been well aware of my connection to her for some time.

The door of the suite was ornately carved like that of a church, and before I had the chance to knock it opened and a liveried servant led me to a dining room as sumptuous as the one downstairs. It was so gloomy outside that even with the curtains wide open the candles were burning, and I despaired of getting anything useful out of my afternoon sittings; Banbury waited at a small table, one eye covered with a bandage stained orange-red with blood. He had already begun to eat his soup and was mopping it up with a crust of bread as I took my seat. "Glad you could come, Bill," he said.

"Thanks for the invitation," I said, and started in on my soup.

"There's no hard feelings about Priscilla, just so you know." As if to mock the room's baroque elegance he was in his shirt-sleeves and what was left of his hair fanned out in all directions as though toweled dry and then neglected by the comb. "Not toward you, anyway."

"I heard you two going at it when I left." A glass of red wine stood next to one of water, which I drained. An elderly man with a waxed moustache appeared at my side and filled it again from a crystal pitcher.

He snorted and tossed the last of his morsel of bread in the remnants of the soup. "Christ, all I said to her was I hoped she wasn't having trouble with bedsores, and the next thing I knew she was shrieking at me, said I was spying on her. I said, 'Priscilla, dear heart, I'm not spying, this is Thursday, same day as I always come by.' Then she's knocked that goddamned curio cabinet of hers on the floor and everything in it's smashed to bits, and then she's got the goddamned fireplace poker in her hand."

"Funny how that bedsores remark didn't restore her equanimity."

"Well, hell, you can't expect me to stand there and say, 'That's all right, sweetheart, you go ahead and lay down for any of my chums your heart desires.' After all I'm paying the goddamned rent on the place." He picked the sodden bread back up and lolled it around in his mouth. "I'd be satisfied if she'd just make a pretense of hiding it from me." He pointed to the bandaged eye. "Now how do you think I explained this to Muriel when I got home?"

"I don't know."

"With considerable goddamned difficulty, is how. Shit, she knows I've got a sweetheart somewhere, but it's a lot easier to pretend when I don't walk in the door with my eye gouged halfway out. I'm lucky not to have lost the goddamned thing."

"I guess you are." Muriel was, in fact, the owner of record of my building, having inherited the entire block from her father, a failed forty-niner who had stumbled upon a vein of silver on his way back east to rejoin his wife and daughter and take a job in his cousin's slaughterhouse in Virginia. I had never met her, as she preferred to keep the more vulgarian of Ralph's companions at arm's length. "How is old Muriel?" I asked, just to be polite.

"She's out of my hair, mostly, getting ready for a big shindig downstairs that's going to cost me a bundle. It's for Gertrude's engagement, did I tell you about that?"

"You didn't. Congratulations."

"Well, he's a young man from Germany, and he's after her mother's money, but at least she'll be out of the house. I love her dearly but Jesus, Mary, and Joseph if she ain't every bit as homely as my own poor Muriel."

The soup was tasty and I was hungry, but I was preoccupied with the thought that Banbury was leading up to a proposal to alter the status quo, which for the moment mostly suited me. The waiter took our soup dishes and put down plates of what looked like bœuf bourguignon, its blackish gravy still bubbling.

"Hell, I've just had a bellyful. That sweet thing she sits on just ain't worth the trouble. What I've been wondering is," he said with his mouth full of the first bite of beef, huffing little breaths in and out to counteract the heat, "how'd you like to take her on full-time?"

I nearly choked on my wine at the thought. "Not much," I said.

"Half the problem's that goddamned laudanum, if you want to know what I think. Fact is," he said, lowering his voice and leaning forward as if afraid Priscilla would hear, "I already got another gal set up here in town and she's not half the trouble Cilla is." Banbury took another bite, blowing on it first.

I placed a forkful of beef into my own mouth, taking the

same precaution and scalding my palate regardless. I wondered if he expected me to keep his plans from Priscilla; I wasn't willing to take up the responsibility of paying her rent, but I thought she should have some warning before she found her means of support removed.

"What's funny is, I used to worry about that husband she left back in Iowa. I wondered if maybe he'd track her down and burst into that bedroom sometime and perforate me." He brought his hand up to his bandaged eye. "And then I figured it out. Hell, he's probably been running the other direction the whole time, worried she's coming after him."

"What do you suppose she'll do without your support?" I said.

"Used to be a seamstress. She could do that again. Wouldn't be able to keep up the way she's living now, but she wouldn't starve. Hell, she could make a living singing."

"Is that a joke?"

He looked puzzled. "You haven't heard her sing and play?"

"Never. Piano's always been shut when I've been there."

He shrugged. "Well, her voice is mighty pretty."

The food was remarkable, and once our conversation turned away from Priscilla I much enjoyed it. Dessert was a sort of bread pudding laced with rum, followed by a very special old pale. Upon finishing Banbury rose, patting his distended abdomen with fond pride. "They serve a hell of a table here," he said.

He walked me downstairs and out to a sidewalk teeming with ill-tempered pedestrians huddled against the cold.

"This gal I got now, she's from the South, a real old-fashioned belle. She orders me around and makes faces and if she doesn't get her way, I don't get mine, if you know what I mean."

"That's the way they are, I understand."

"The damnedest thing is, I like it. She hardly even makes an affectation of liking me, and yet I come back." He coughed into his fist, trying hard to get something out of his throat. "Well, I sure wish you'd think this over. I'd hate like hell to see Priscilla thrown out onto the street."

"You'll keep paying the rent for a few months, won't you? Until she can find something?"

He looked at me as if I were insane. "Christ, supporting three women in three different houses is about to put me in the goddamn alms house." He walked away, shaking his head, and gave a little wave without looking back.

HAVING A LITTLE time to spare I walked blocks out of my way with my hands in my coat pockets, prodding with my tongue a little flap of skin that dangled, heat-shredded, from the roof of my mouth. At Nineteenth Street I turned right and headed to Market Street, thinking I might find Augie there. Since one or more of my afternoon sittings seemed likely to cancel on me I thought I might as well conduct my business with him and be done with it, but walking up the street I was importuned a dozen times without seeing any trace of him.

One of these unfortunates approached me with a smile of recognition on her face. "Well, it's old Sean Cooney from Boston, ain't it? It's me, Mary Dolan, from up the street." Her face was worn by drink and laudanum and hard luck, but there was nonetheless a sweet softness to her aspect that suggested a kindly soul; in easier circumstances and with better dentition she would have been pretty. "I always liked you better than your brother; he's got a mean streak like your old man did."

"I'm not him," I said.

"The hell you ain't. What say you and me go back there to Boston for that centennial celebration? This Denver business ain't working so good for me as I'd imagined it would."

"I'm not him, and the centennial was last year besides."

"Like hell it was."

"1776 plus one hundred equals 1876. Two years ago."

"The hell you say."

"It's a fact. Don't you remember the Fourth of July? All the fireworks and the parade?"

"Go on with you, they have those every year on the Fourth of July!"

"So they do," I said, and resumed walking.

She followed me. "Say, Seanny. Remember that milliner's I worked for? Mrs. So-and-So? You think she'd take me back on?"

She wasn't going to accept the fact that I wasn't Sean Cooney, and I hesitated to give life-altering counsel to a stranger, but clearly Denver wasn't doing her any favors. "I'd say if you want to go back to Boston, though, you ought to give it a try." Satisfied, she nodded and turned away from me, and I made my escape.

I NEXT MADE a detour in the direction of picturesque Hop Alley, thinking I might pick up the day's laundry and save Mrs. Fenster a trip. I had no idea which of the dozen or more launderers was hers, however, and I walked past without stopping to check any of them. The signage on the street was in both English and Chinese, and I noted three more or less respectable-looking white ladies knock, giggling, at the door of one particular business with no outward identification but a painted number 531 and a vertical quartet of Chinese characters. The man who answered maintained his poker face but let them in, glancing momentarily at me as though daring me to object. I had nothing against what they were up to, though; to my way of thinking it was on par with Priscilla's laudanum-taking, and I reminded myself to stop at the pharmacist's to pick up a replacement bottle for my next visit to Golden.

AUGIE DIDN'T SHOW up that afternoon, and neither did two of three scheduled sitters, and I sent the third home for lack of illumination. I used the freed-up time to go over my books and, later, to examine Augie's samples and catalogues. I was already overstocked on most subjects: the War, Geography, the Sciences, Great Personalities, and Comic Scenes, and browsing through the catalogue I saw at first nothing listed that inspired me to add to the inventory. Then my eye stopped at a new listing:

OGDEN & GLEASON, PHOTOGRAPHERS, COTTONWOOD, KANS.

This came as a shock, seeing my own former moniker and hometown in print. I was pleased nonetheless to note that young Gleason had kept the business going. The set of pictures advertised was titled "Scenes of the Former Osage Territory," described merely as "a series of artistically conceived views of the recently tamed wilderness, incl. a two-headed goat and a white buffalo calf, and the murder cabin belonging to the notorious Benders."

The day after Maggie and I escaped from Cottonwood I felt the first vague pangs of regret for the vanished opportunity to make a stereographic record of the Bender house and property for publication; I was thus gratified to see that young Gleason had seized it, doubly so that he'd left my name on the business, since taking it off the shingle would doubtless have pleased many in town. I marked down an order for a set.

The sun never showed itself that afternoon, and I sat in the studio and read until six. Mrs. Fenster had sent the boy out for a slab of bacon, and when he returned with it she began cooking a portion of it up with some beans. I withdrew to the studio to resume my reading, and a few minutes later I returned to the kitchen to find Lemuel still there, to the great annoyance of his aunt.

"Says he's hungry," she said, as if the claim were the height of absurdity.

"Didn't you feed him at noon?"

She drew herself up to her full five feet. "You said there was to be no luncheon."

"Better give him some bacon and beans, then." The boy had already taken his place at table, and after serving me my portion and filling a plate for herself Mrs. Fenster dipped her ladle into the cook pot with exaggerated reluctance and loaded a plate for him.

I wasn't overly hungry owing to the rich meal I'd taken at midday, and Mrs. Fenster ate in her usual dainty manner, but the boy fed as though he hadn't eaten a morsel in days. When I commented benignly on the urgency of his eating he stopped, wide-eyed, for a moment.

"Didn't mean nothing. Sorry." He put his fork down.

"Why'd you stop? Go on, eat. Your aunt'll fix up some more if your belly's as empty as that."

After a cautious moment he decided I wasn't japing and set

about eating again. I had the old woman fry a bit more bacon, and she added it with some more brown, crusty beans to his plate. He tore into that with the same breathtaking gusto as he had his first portion, and the gluttonous spectacle had begun to tickle me.

"Care for a third helping?"

He nodded warily, and she fried him still more bacon. There was another plate's worth of beans in the pot, too, and he finished that off as well before letting loose with a belch that would have shocked a muleskinner. After shooting a worried glance at Mrs. Fenster he grinned sheepishly at my laughter, and nearly an hour after his usual departure time he went out the door for home. I sat up for a while, reading and ruminating on the world of separation between a resourceful farm boy like Horace Gleason, capable of replacing me completely at a technically demanding craft after but a few months training, and a dull city boy like poor Lemuel, incapable even of mustering the nerve to trouble his own aunt for a meal that he was due as a condition of his employment.

THE NEXT MORNING was sunny, and I busied myself on the rooftop printing what I should have done the day before. At eleven o'clock I had to go downstairs and wait for Augie Baxter myself, since Lemuel hadn't come in that morning. Though he'd never before failed to arrive on time I was more angry than concerned, having had to perform most of the lad's chores in addition to my own. When Augie arrived I was in an unusually foul temper; as I'd anticipated he complained bitterly at my puny order and then proceeded to criticize the one new addition to it.

"We just added them back in January. Pretty pictures, to be sure, the fellow's got a sharp eye. There's not much remarkable about that set, though."

"I see there's a view of the Bender cabin," I said with as much casual indifference as I could manage.

"Well, a few years ago we were selling a full set of those, but they were a disappointment. Just one skeleton was all you could see, and a few pictures of buildings and a bunch of yahoos standing in front of some holes in the ground and some trees on fire. What it really needed is a view of them Benders hung from a tree, then you'd have something you could sell."

I thought of something just then: the nude views I'd taken of Maggie, the ones I'd had to leave behind in Cottonwood. "This fellow Gleason, he doesn't handle any views of naked ladies, does he?"

"Naw, not that I seen, anyway. I think he's got religion. And speaking of naked ladies, you missed yourself a free roll in the hay yesternoon." He leaned back in his armchair, looking quite pleased with himself.

After Augie left I sat alone in the gallery and imagined discreetly contacting Horace Gleason and seeing if he had those views of Maggie. If I couldn't trust young Gleason, who'd been upstanding enough to keep my name on his business after my disgrace, whom could I trust?

My answer came quickly and harshly; I was prosperous, well-respected, and suspected of nothing, after years of fear and penury. Wagering my liberty, my neck, and my hard-won money on Gleason's good nature was out of the question, no matter how badly I wanted those pictures back. I would continue to call them forth, imperfect, from memory, and be glad I could do that.

It was nearly noon, and I hadn't yet read the morning newspapers, and I thought I'd seek out the *News* to read with my midday meal. I put on my hat and started to leave, and as I started down the steps the front door opened to reveal my young assistant standing in the center of its frame, appearing even smaller than usual. My first inclination, having spent most of the morning angry with him, was to yell, but his face was so pallid and drawn I stopped myself before a sound came out. He held the door open with his left leg instead of his hand, which dangled strangely at his side, and over his right shoulder he carried a bindle tied to the end of a stick. Without undue harshness I asked what had kept him.

"Sorry, Mister," he said, and his voice broke on the first syllable. "I think I'll be having to quit on account of my arm." It broke again on "arm."

"What's the matter with your arm?" I asked, and I took hold of the door and motioned him inside.

"It's pretty sore," he said when we got to the top of the stairs. It certainly looked that way from where I stood.

"How'd that happen?"

He looked down at the parquet. "It was the smell's what it was."

"What smell?" I asked, exasperated at his lack of eloquence.

"The farting. My old man got tired of it after a while and he cracked me a couple good ones."

"Jesus. Your pa did that over a little gas?"

"It was a lot of gas," he said.

I called for Mrs. Fenster and she waddled in carrying a rag. She scowled at the sight of the boy, as though his unreliability reflected poorly on her.

"The lad's hurt his arm," I said.

She sniffed and threw her rag over her shoulder and roughly tugged his sleeve upward. "You're long past due for your bathing, young man," she said, and if she was about to add some other insulting comment, she stopped at the sight of his arm, which displayed a nascent rainbow of skin tones from red to black, with orange predominating, the yellows and purples yet to add themselves to the ghastly palette.

"Lay that bindle down there and we'll go see Ernie Stickhammer down the street." I beckoned him to follow me down the stairs.

"Sawbones costs money," Mrs. Fenster yelled from the top of the stairs, as though fearing that any moment I might come to my senses and leave her or the boy responsible for Stickhammer's fee.

"Don't trouble yourself, Mrs. Fenster," I called up to her. "Stickhammer's the cheapest doctor in Colorado."

Ernie Stickhammer was an unmarried native of Montreal, Canada, and lived in a small room in the back of his office, which occupied three rooms six doors down the street from the gallery, up a comically narrow flight of stairs.

"You sure about seeing the doc?" the boy asked, as though I had suggested an audience with the president or the pope of Rome and not a dipsomaniac provincial sawbones. We waited in a small antechamber for him to be done with another patient, and after a few minutes Stickhammer came out in his shirtsleeves in the company of a man with a nose the size of a gherkin, the texture of a cauliflower, and the queasy purplish gray hue of an eggplant. The man left without any words exchanged between him and the doctor, who shook his head sadly after him.

"And what have we here?"

The doctor sported blond whiskers down to his chin, and his face was such a bright pink Lemuel couldn't help staring at it as he led the boy into the consultation room and helped him up onto a table. Stickhammer's notice had already been drawn to the boy's mangled limb, and he knelt to examine it, gingerly pulling the worn sleeve away without causing the boy undue pain.

"My helper's busted his arm." I myself wouldn't have brought any medical problem as challenging as the previous patient's enlarged nose to Stickhammer, but he'd do for setting a broken arm.

The light of day shining through the window of the room showed to better advantage the discolored, traumatized flesh that extended from shoulder to elbow. The arm was scarred with old wounds as well, more or less healed, including what looked like a bad burn at the shoulder, and I hated to think what the rest of him looked like uncovered. "Sweet Christ almighty." Stickhammer looked up at me. "You didn't do this to him, did you?"

"Hell, no. His old man did it."

"He did, eh? How old are you, lad?"

"Eighteen," Lemuel said after a moment's thought, surprising the doctor and me both. I'd have taken him for thirteen or so.

"And why'd the old boy find it necessary to crack your arm this way?"

"Got the farts pretty awful and couldn't quit."

Stickhammer nodded, as though that were a common cause of such injuries. "All right, let's get this old shirt off of you, boy."

At that I turned to leave. "How much to set it, Ernie?"

"Two-fifty," he said, and, smarting a bit myself, I left two silver dollars and a half on his desk and told the boy to come back over when he was all done. As I descended the front staircase I winced at the sound of the boy crying out in pain at the shirt's removal.

A ROAST CHICKEN was ready when I returned to the studio, and by the time Mrs. Fenster and I had done eating the boy had returned with his newly splinted arm in a canvas sling, the empty sleeve of his ragged shirt hanging, slit in half, at his side.

"Pay you back," he said as he started eating, though we all knew he couldn't reasonably do so any time soon.

"You can work it off," I said. "It's a good thing he busted the left and not the right."

He gaped at me, slack-jawed, then down at his arm as though trying to remember what had happened to it, then back up at me. "Can't work. Arm's broke."

"That's why nature gave you two of them. There's plenty of one-armed men my age who've been working for a living since the war."

He nodded, not understanding my point but eager to please.

"All right, then, why don't you start preparing the plates for the one o'clock sitting," I said.

"Yes, sir," he said, and he started for the darkroom, very slowly.

"Did Stickhammer give you something for that pain?" I asked, suddenly afraid I would have to do all the afternoon's work myself after all.

"How do you mean?"

"Did he give you a drink to make the hurting stop?"

"Yes, sir," he said in a somnambulist's molasses-thick murmur. I should have thought to tell Stickhammer not to dope him up, but I hadn't, and for my neglect I found myself saddled with a one-armed, opiated imbecile for a helper.

I had to assist him with all his tasks that afternoon, right down to mixing up the collodion, and by day's end I despaired of his ever relearning the work one-handed. At the end of the day Mrs. Fenster called me aside.

"Where's the boy to stay tonight?" she asked.

"At home," I said, seeing no reason he shouldn't, as long as he wasn't farting.

"At home with that man what did that to him?" she said. "No thank you, Mr. Sadlaw. Here's the place for him. I'll fix him up a bed in the studio and unmake it first thing in the morning. You won't even know he's here."

"Because he won't be." I got quite enough of Lemuel in the daytime, and the truth was that Mrs. Fenster was one too many members of my household already.

"He'll stay for the time being. Till I can get something else arranged."

Her impertinence was as unusual as the concern she showed the boy, who most days annoyed her more than he did me, and I was so surprised I acquiesced. She set about preparing a makeshift bed for him in the studio on the canapé. He stared at the bed, transfixed, nodding slightly as she explained to him the overnight rules of the house, rules she was making up as she did so, as none of them applied to me or her. He was still contemplating the bed with a long strand of drool hanging from his lower lip and a dullness to his eye when I left them.

THE STRAINS OF the afternoon's unassisted labors called for release. My back and shoulders were as stiff and sore as if I had spent the day hammering railroad spikes, and my anger and frustration, with no legitimate target but a half-crippled idiot, were ready to overflow. I stepped out onto the street with no precise idea of where I would end the evening, but when I chose a direction it was toward the stables on the street behind. I knew what it would take to restore my peace of mind, at least for the night.

AS I HAD on several previous occasions stepping up to Priscilla's front door, I spied one of her neighbors scowling through her front parlor window at me. She was young and rather pretty, and on several occasions I had seen her with children of varying ages. Her expression was so vituperative I laughed out loud, and if not for the pane of glass between us she might have spat at me. She looked like she did it often enough to be good at it, and might have hit me even at that distance.

When the door opened Priscilla eyed me with only slightly more friendliness than her neighbor. It was well past the hour at which she stopped accepting unannounced callers, but I hoped she might break her rule this once. "Look what the wind blew over," she said.

"I wondered if you might be free to dine with me," I said.

"I've already eaten, like any normal person has by this hour. Why don't you come in, anyhow."

As we lay there a while later, she said, "Someone told me you and Ralph dined together. So you needn't worry about concealing it."

For a moment I wondered if her informant was the waiter, but he had overheard the entire exchange, and if he were betraying confidences he surely wouldn't have stopped there. "That's true," I said, feeling a little glum and disloyal for not revealing to her the nature of my conversation with Banbury. The opportunities open to a woman her age weren't many or attractive, and the odds of finding another patron as generous as Banbury were slim, regardless of her beauty or the advanced level of her intimate skills; youth was generally the chief attribute a rich old buzzard wanted hanging from his arm, even when its possessor was only halfway to pretty. Priscilla had been a dressmaker back in Iowa, though, and I supposed she might still make a living at that somewhere.

"I hope you weren't negotiating for my favors without my participation," she said, rolling slightly toward me to afford a better view of her lovely sex, its labia dark and glistening, a microscopically thin strand of semen suspended delicately across the hairy canopy just above it. The faint odor of recent copulation intoxicated me at that moment like morphine; there wasn't much I would have refused her then, and I hoped she wouldn't press for too many details. "We talked about you only in context of your grace and beauty."

She laughed and was quiet for a moment as she rolled back against the mattress and rolled toward me, noting my gaze fixed on *l'origine du monde*. "And how are you faring, Mr. Sadlaw, generally?"

"I'm too busy lately, having as I do only half an assistant." I described to her the circumstances of Lemuel's injury, to her anger and indignation. I reminded her that she didn't even know the boy, which placated her not at all.

She rose up and leaned on her arm so that her breasts hung down slantways, their nipples still rosy and swollen. "Charges should be brought."

"I don't know that they could, under the circumstances. I guess a father's got the right to punish his own son. Anyway, I don't know that the boy'd testify against his pa like that."

"Then you should do it. He's your employee, after all, and your trade will suffer for it. Surely the police would understand that. Ralph has plenty of contacts among the police."

I just nodded. Her righteous vehemence aroused me, and her too, judging by the ardor with which she responded to the pressure of my lips against hers. Soon I was astride her again, and this one was so long in extinguishing itself that I asked to stay the night, which I'd never done there before; she turned me down flat, for the sake of the neighbors, who might think the less of her for it.

THREE

Cut Down by a Lady

After my father's suicide one of my well-intentioned but busy uncles thought to distract me from my bewildered grief with a dog. I named her Ginger, though her coat was salt-and-pepper, after a dog my father and I had both been fond of. I remembered being sent out into the lady's garden to play with that first Ginger many an afternoon while my father and the dog's mistress, Mrs. Merryvale, discussed spiritual matters inside the house.

My own Ginger was a mutt whose previous owner had died. As a result of his regularly administered beatings she was slightly lame and terrified of all adult males and many females as well, and though eventually she grew less skittish she only really ever trusted children. Though she never mastered any of the rudiments of canine dressage she was so sweet-natured and eager for affection that no one much cared about her failures in deportment, and she was well-loved by the neighborhood boys and girls, many of whom associated with the son of a suicide only because of her. Working with the idiot I was sometimes reminded of Ginger; it was as easy to forgive him cracking an exposed plate as it was to pardon her urinating in the parlor when we forgot to let her out (for she never learned that a bark would grant her egress). There was the same look in the eye of abject sorrow and culpability, of the certainty of swift and terrible punishment, of grateful astonishment when it didn't come. If I hadn't come to like him, precisely, I tolerated his presence well enough and had stopped contemplating his replacement with a more useful helper.

AFTER A FEW days Lem was able to perform most of his tasks without the aid of his useless left arm but they went slowly, and when we were rushed I had to help him. He complained hardly at all about the hurt in his arm and generally spoke even less than he normally did. He continued to sleep in the studio, and I made no effort to find him new lodgings. Sleeping there he was able to start his workday earlier, which compensated slightly for his slowness, and I was scarcely aware of his presence anyway.

It occurred to me that since he no longer had to turn over his wages to his tyrant of a father, and had no living expenses to speak of, he must have been socking some money away, and I asked him about it one afternoon as we stocked the darkroom, and he answered without hesitation or shame.

"I squirrel some away. Some I spend, now's I got it."

"What do you have to spend it on, with free meals and a roof over your head?"

"Hoors, Mr. Sadlaw. I go down to one of the fancy houses yonder on Market Street."

I burst out laughing, which puzzled him.

"Didn't want to bring 'em here," he said, helpfully. "Wouldn't want to screw on the couch, there, where people get their picture made. And my auntie wouldn't like it much, I don't guess."

I began to suspect that some of that salary was also going toward the purchase of morphine injections from Dr. Stickhammer, who seemed very well-informed regarding Lemuel's progress despite the fact that I had not taken him back in since the day the arm was set. The boy was so addled under normal circumstances that it was hard to tell from his speech and demeanor whether he was hopped up or not, but frequently after his midday meal break—which he no longer took with Mrs. Fenster and me—he returned to the studio with his pupils dilated and his manner especially dreamy and contented. I thought of trying to curtail it but it didn't seem right; soon enough, I reasoned, the arm would be healed and he could quit the stuff.

His unskilled duties had increased as his ability to perform his few skilled ones had diminished, and these now included fetching the morning newspapers for breakfast. One Monday morning as his aunt toiled in the kitchen he laid the *Bulletin*, the *Daily Times*, the *Call*, the *Tribune,* and the *Rocky Mountain News* down on the breakfast table. Neither of us said anything, and I was well into the *Bulletin* when he retreated into the kitchen for a word with Mrs. Fenster. I might have warned him that she was in an unusually foul temper that day, but I was absorbed by the news of the day and anyway didn't much care what the old termagant did to him. I was examining the advertisements on the third page when the boy exited the kitchen and stood next to me for half a minute, saying nothing.

"Are you lacking in work to do today?" I asked. "Because if so, I can think of a dozen jobs that need starting."

"No, sir. Could you read me something from out of there?"

Taken aback, I asked what he wanted to learn about.

"Anything in there about a man got shot in front of a saloon yesterday?"

The article was on the front page, and I began reading it:

CUT DOWN BY A LADY

HIS ASSAILANT'S IDENTITY YET TO BE DISCOVERED.

The Bulletin's Own Pressman—
A Model Employee for Three Years—
Devoted Husband and Father of Four—
He Is Not Expected to Last the Day.

At about eleven o'clock last night Hiram Cowan, a printing press operator for the *Bulletin*, stepped out of the Silver Star Saloon near our offices, at whose door he was met by either one woman or two, depending upon the witness telling the tale, and shot through the abdomen with a small pistol. Mr. Cowan fell to the ground, whereupon his assailant or assailants fled into the darkness. Although the finest in medical care has been provided for him he is not expected to see the sun set again.

Members of the Denver Police expressed confidence that an arrest of the murderer can be made by this afternoon at the latest, and that with luck the victim will live sufficiently long to identify his killer.

I put the paper down and found that the boy wasn't listening. His gaze was fixed at the ground, and his left foot skidded back and forth in a slow rhythm. He looked as close to thoughtful as I had ever seen him.

"That mean he's dead or ain't?"

"Sounds like he's going to be, soon enough. Did you see it happen?"

He looked up at me, his breath whistling softly through his half-open mouth. "Nuh-uh."

"What's your interest, then?"

"That's my old man."

I glanced at the article again. I had failed to recognize the father's name, I realized, because I'd never bothered to learn the boy's surname. I was surprised to learn that his father was employed, since I'd been under the impression that Lemuel was the family's sole source of income, and I said so.

"I mostly am, since he don't bring much home with him."

He didn't look very sad about his old pa's impending demise. "Do you want to go and see him?"

He shook his head no. "Not particular."

BETWEEN THE PRIVY and the stable the odor in the summertime was faint-making, but on this chilly afternoon the ammoniac smell that wafted upward was ever present but faint, more like the memory of the stench than the thing itself. The sensation was almost pleasant, calling to mind long-ago Ohio mornings puzzling apart the most rudimentary of the classical texts before the curiosity-killing drudgery of the school day began.

Now I sat browsing through the *Rocky Mountain News* in the angular light that leaked down through the cracks between the rough pine boards of the shabbily constructed outhouse around that time of day. When I had finished I put the paper into the rack I had fashioned for storage of reading materials and pulled from it that morning's already perused *Bulletin*, whose front page, with its account of the shooting of Lem's Pa, I tore into strips and rendered illegible.

My schedule for the afternoon was clear of obligations and appointments, and my plans vague. I didn't relish the thought of languishing in the gallery, ordering the boy about and waiting for clients who likely would never materialize, but I hated the thought of missing any who might unexpectedly wander in. I stepped out squinting into the last white light the courtyard would receive that day, and my thoughts went straight to the prints languorously revealing themselves on the rooftop: a sweet elderly lady brought in by her granddaughter for her first photograph, shriveled as a dried-out apple and peering into the lens as though into Satan's eyeball with an expression wholly unlike the kindly one she'd worn upon entry; a glum lad of sixteen or so trying to make himself out as a dandy, who had required assistance in knotting his silk cravat and in combing his shaggy hair into a poet's wild mane; and finally one of the broomstick madam's young ladies, who had come in with her patroness wanting to have a portrait made for the parents of a young client who had taken a strong liking to and wanted to marry her, one that would make her look like a lady. As I began to ascend I looked upward to find Lemuel peering anxiously down at me from the edge of the rooftop, and I assumed he was waiting for his turn to go down and void his bladder.

"Hold your horses, I'll be up in a moment," I told him, but when I reached the top he didn't take the ladder.

"A man brought a box by and he's waiting to be paid." This simple turn of events completely stymied him, and the thought of paying the man from the cashbox never entered his inch-thick blond skull. I took a moment to check on the progress of the prints, which to my satisfaction were about exactly far along as I'd calculated, then climbed down the other ladder into the foyer and found a very angry messenger waiting on the piano bench. He was the size of a stevedore and spoke like a fallen schoolmaster.

"I hope your bowel enjoyed a satisfactory evacuation," he said, "having cost me as it did goddamn near a quarter of an hour." An enormous moustache like a horse brush covered his mouth completely, and just above and below it on the left side could be seen the ends of a gruesome scar the lip cover was doubtless meant to hide. Like Lemuel he had only one useful arm, his left; the right was lost entirely. Idly I pondered whether its severing had been concurrent to receiving the scar on his mouth, and I ignored his insolent tone in favor of providing the boy with a valuable lesson.

"You see, Lem?" I said, gesturing at the empty sleeve. "This fellow's down to one arm permanently, and he hasn't let it slow him any."

Lemuel stared with mute terror as the man stood, scowling at me, and recited bitterly the price owed on delivery. I paid him from the billfold in my vest and took the package. The messenger left without further comment, and before I had a chance to open the package the street-side door opened again. A pair of drunks stumbled up the staircase and into the foyer, laughing.

"I would like to get my picture taken with my bosom chum, here, Mr. Schuster," one of them said. He was the bigger of the two, but they were both big. He was jug-eared and square of jaw, and I had the idea that, sober, he was probably stern of countenance and not inclined to such impulsive behavior as getting your picture taken in the middle of the afternoon.

Mr. Schuster just stood there, looking around at the foyer, drunker than his companion and only dimly aware, I thought, of the nature of his visit. They had money, to judge by their new-looking clothes, and appeared willing to part with it lightheartedly, so I led them into the studio and ordered the boy into the darkroom to make ready the plates for a full portrait session, with *cartes de visite* and eight-by-twelve-inch single and double sittings. I suspected they wouldn't even remember they'd had the pictures made, much less where to pick up the proofs, so I would charge them an up-front fee for a *de luxe* sitting. I spent the better part of two hours with them, trying to get them to settle down enough for a sharp exposure, and when they were done I hurried them out the door, doubtful I would ever see them again. I'd print up a set of proofs just in case, but they would almost certainly have left Denver before they remembered their picture had been made, much less where they'd had it done.

Mrs. Fenster returned from Hop Alley with the day's clean linen and informed me that she had procured me a client. "The old Chinee owns the laundry and about eight other things down there, his nephew's going to bring him down tomorrow for a picture. He's good for a bunch of *cartes de visite* to send home to China, and probably a big one too for the laundry wall."

"I'm much obliged, Mrs. Fenster."

"That's all right. He gives me the eye, you know, when I go in." She put her hand to her enormous hip with her elbow jutted outward, and raised an eyebrow.

"Is that so," I said, striving to keep the doubt and mirth out of my voice.

"Oh, it's all right. Long's we can make a little money off of him."

"Of course."

WHEN THE SUN was low in the sky I took a walk with the laughable notion of getting some fresh air into my lungs; laughable because a layer of fog and smoke hung over the entire Denver basin like a doused campfire as it did on any moist day cold enough for fires to be built. It was getting colder as I made my way downtown and entered Schrafft's Biergarten, where a large crowd had already gathered to celebrate the passage of another workday. A tiny orchestra played music on the bandstand, and the few women present were dancing in front of it with those men bold enough to have asked first. Standing at the bar I searched the crowd for a friend but saw none; I ordered a beer, then asked the barman if there was an errand boy on the premises. I slapped down a whole dime, since this was the better sort of beer hall, and the bartender slid a mugful down the slick bar. After a sip I composed a note on a piece of scrap in my vest pocket, and a moment later a boy not much bigger than Lemuel stood before me. Feeling expansive, I gave him a whole quarter and strict instructions to hand the note to no one but Ralph Banbury at the *Bulletin*.

The hall was filling up and growing noisier, and while there was still room I took a seat at one of the long tables that ran its length. Nursing at my beer and watching the crowd as the sky grew dark and the gaslights came on, I thought how many friends I would have found stepping into my old saloon in Cottonwood, and how few I had in this townful of friendly acquaintances. I consoled myself with the thought that I was making a good living and concentrated on the loveliness of the dancing girls, who waltzed now to a quick tempo. One of them in particular caught my fancy and lifted my spirits, a fair-haired belle without much skill as a dancer who laughed good-naturedly at her every misstep.

I imagined she was German by birth, as were a large percentage of the clientele, and noted a wisp of loose hair, *frisé* and pale as wheat straw, that she kept sweeping back from the left side of her forehead with a slightly irritated half smirk at whichever fellow she was dancing with at the moment. By the time she was on her fourth partner that wisp was dark, slicked to her temple with sweat; I had half determined that I would approach her and take a slot on her dance card when it came to me that my attraction was founded on her slight resemblance to my own absent Maggie. I remained seated, watching her with my hat discreetly on my lap.

I might have gone home if not for the invitation I'd extended to Banbury, but the boy returned shortly—the *Bulletin*'s offices were just two blocks away—and reported that Mr. Banbury would join me within the half hour. I took a seat with my beer and drank it slowly, growing ever more morose with every tune the orchestra played and with every whirl the dancer I'd fancied made on the dance floor.

WHEN BANBURY ARRIVED he slapped me on the back and set two beers down on the long table in front of us. He had on a brown bowler, and the bandage over his eye was gone. That eye itself was barely discernible between its swollen purple and black lids, but the other was wrinkled with merriment. "You cheap son of a bitch," he said. "I assumed you'd be buying the suds." He took a long swig from his glass and belched.

"How's your eye?" I asked, and took a last drink from my first glass and then another from the fresh one.

"Better than it was," he said. "I hate like hell having to lie every goddamn time somebody asks me about it, though."

"Tell them you've been set upon by irate subscribers again."

He took out two cigars, clipped them both, and handed me one. He looked up toward the bandstand, where a polka tune had just ended. "Jesus, Bill, do you see the one in the blue dress?" he said, jerking his head toward my dancer. She was just sitting down on a bench next to her last dance partner, and they shared a kiss and clasped hands as the band started anew.

"You change your mind about Cilla?" He licked some beer foam off of his moustache and then took a puff. "I'm going to keep up payments through the end of the lease in July, and then she's out."

"Hell, Ralph, I can't afford to keep a woman in a separate lodging."

"You're a bachelor. She can move in with you and nobody'll know she's not your wife."

"I don't want to live with her, for God's sake." I took a puff on the cigar. It was a good one, better than I'd had in a long time. "Have you told her yet?"

He pushed his hat back to give his forehead some air. "No, and don't you either. As long as I'm paying for that place, I'm going to get me a piece of ass once a week, and I don't want to have to worry about her stabbing me in the midst of it."

"That's a lovely sentiment."

"Don't be high and mighty. Remember you'll be getting at least as much of that as me until then, and on my nickel, besides."

We watched the dancers for a minute in silence.

"Say," he said. "How's that Mrs. Fenster?"

"She's all right."

"You know, her brother-in-law got shot last night. One of my pressmen, that's how I came to know her in the first place."

"I heard someone got him outside the Silver Star."

"That's right. Gutshot the son of a bitch, and from what I hear nobody's crying about it. We're making him out in the paper to be a saint, since it sells a few more copies. All the wife wanted to know when she heard about it was how the hell were they going to pay their bills with him gone. I guess he beat the shit out of her pretty regular, and the kids too. I was there at Doc Marcy's this afternoon, and I heard her say to him, 'Not such a hard one now, are you, Cowan?' "

"His boy works for me, and he's not too broken up about it, either. The old man busted his arm not long ago."

He nodded and chewed on his cigar. "Supposed to be a woman that did it. I was wondering myself if it wasn't the older boy, the little squirrely one. He works for you?"

"He couldn't have done it, he's timid as a runt kitten."

"Better watch that boy," he said. He drained the remainder of beer in the glass in a single draught and slapped my shoulder again. "Sorry this has to be brief, old pal, but I have a rendezvous with a dainty little magnolia flower, and your summons provided a lovely excuse to leave the office early." He tipped his hat and meandered off, the closest thing I had in the world to a friend right then, with the sole, possible exception of the woman we were both about to betray.

DINNER THAT EVENING was chicken with gravy and dumplings, and a baked potato in its jacket, superfluous alongside the dumplings but delicious filled with the chicken gravy. When it was gone I felt quite inflated and was debating with myself the merits of a stroll for digestive purposes when I heard a rapping at the front door. I didn't hear Mrs. Fenster grumbling about it and so assumed that she was downstairs at the johnny, and I descended the stairs myself to find Priscilla on the landing, dressed as if for church services or a fancy ball.

"May I come in?" she asked, and I stepped aside to let her pass, and the ruffling and scratching of her skirts as she hastily ascended made me forget my postprandial walk.

I showed her a quick tour of the studio and gallery. When she stretched out on the davenport in an inviting pose I informed her that it was the bed of my idiot helper, who would likely be returning soon from Market Street and his friends there. Her expression shifted imperceptibly from wanton to demure and she straightened herself. After a moment she rose, wiping her hands on her dress.

"Perhaps there's somewhere else we could have a lie-down?"

I led her to my bedroom, and as luck would have it we crossed Mrs. Fenster on the way there. "Good night, Mr. Sadlaw. Sleep well," was all she said, with no discernible sarcasm.

As we entered my room I began unbuttoning my vest, and Priscilla pulled me to her. "Never mind undressing, just lift my skirts and give it to me quick."

It was only now that I saw, and smelled, how much she'd had to drink, most likely on top of a goodly dose of laudanum. I ran my hand under her skirts and underskirts and found her legs above her stockings bare; a quick application of my fingertips at their juncture confirmed that she had already performed most of the preliminary work of arousal herself. I followed her instructions and screwed her standing and from behind. When I was done we fell onto the bed, fully clothed down to our shoes except for my prick hanging at half-mast from my trousers.

"That was just the thing, Bill," she said.

"Good," I said. We lay in silence for a while, and then I thought of my earlier interview with Banbury. "Don't you usually entertain my landlord Monday evenings?"

It was a moment before she answered, and her voice quavered slightly when she did. "He sent word this morning he couldn't come. I came to town to see if I couldn't catch him in a lie, or maybe change his mind."

"Did you find him?"

"No." She was quiet for a minute. "I'm so afraid he's with that bitch of a wife." She sobbed out loud, and it went on for a few minutes. When she stopped she rolled over and kissed me, and started unbuttoning my vest. Five minutes later we were naked, and doing it as it was meant to be done, and the whole time I kept telling myself I had to tell her the truth. But we went to sleep without talking any more, and in the morning it seemed once again like a bad idea.

AT EIGHT THIRTY a.m. I sat at the breakfast table alone. Priscilla had elected to return home rather than face Mrs. Fenster at table, and as soon as my coffee and eggs arrived the boy entered with the morning papers.

"Heard some yelling when I come home last night," he said. "Sounded like a gal."

"Never you mind about that," I said, and I grabbed the *Bulletin* from the top of the pile. His father was on the front page again:

COWAN YET LIVES

THE GUNMAN STILL AT LARGE—POLICE HOPEFUL THE *BULLETIN*'S STRICKEN PRESSMAN WILL AWAKEN AND NAME HIS ATTACKER—HIS WIFE AND CHILDREN AT HIS BEDSIDE, KNEELING IN PRAYER.

His Survival a Miracle, Says Doctor Marcy—
More Eye-Witnesses Interviewed—
Say Two Women Were the Assassins.

Only yesterday morning the case of Hiram Cowan, a printing press operator for the *Bulletin* shot down in the street on the night of the 10th, was given up as hopeless and funerary arrangements were being contemplated. Yet sundown and dawn both found him clinging valiantly to existence, and there is now reason to hope that he may recover entirely. He is now under the care of Dr. Hamilton Marcy, whose services have been engaged by the *Bulletin*.

I LOOKED UP over the edge of the paper at Lemuel and noticed Mrs. Fenster standing in the kitchen doorway behind him. The boy looked dispassionately at me. "So he ain't dead?"

"Not yet," I said. "Says down here they're paying all your ma's expenses in the meantime."

"How come?"

"It's a gesture to their readers more than to your family. It makes them look Christian and kind."

Mrs. Fenster gave a snort like a rhinoceros. "It's all because it's a good story, their own pressman getting shot in the street.

If he was accidentally run down by a wagon you can bet they'd have let him die there in the street and found a new pressman in a hurry." There was a note of disappointment in her voice that this wasn't the case.

"You know, Lem, I could take you down to the paper and introduce you to the editor. Maybe you could get a little money out of him."

"No, sir, I don't care to do that." He shook his head and left the room to start his work.

THE AFTERNOON'S SITTINGS went smoothly, including the one with the owner of the laundry. The nephew who accompanied him spoke excellent English, and though he was formally deferential toward both his uncle and I, his expression was sullen to the point of hostility. I took no offense, particularly, as I decided to interpret it as an Eastern form of politeness; the uncle was so polite he addressed not so much as a glance to me except through the intermediary of the lens as I focused his upside-down image first in the eight-by-twelve and then the *carte de visite* camera. He had ordered sets of both, as Mrs. Fenster had predicted, and she made several excuses to enter the studio during the sitting, fluttering coquettishly about and trying to attract the attention of the old man, who might as well have been alone in the room. He was dressed in a magnificent black silk shirt that came down to his knees, with a pair of snakelike dragons embroidered on its front, and a single enormous one on the back. His trousers and a small, round, flat-topped hat were made of the same silk, and the pointed toes of his slippers were just visible beneath the trouser legs. When the sitting was finished the younger man bowed and bid us farewell, and the old man deigned to bow silently. I returned the bow with a short speech, and the younger man seemed satisfied with the correctness of the gesture.

"He's a very important fellow down there in Hop Alley," Mrs. Fenster said, nodding at me as she made for the kitchen. She had come out to say good-bye, and neither the old man nor the nephew had acknowledged her verbally or otherwise, but I had an odd sensation that outside my presence she and the old man were quite friendly.

FOUR

SKULLDUGGERY!

That evening after dinner Mrs. Fenster asked if she could have the rest of the evening off, as her sister was feeling poorly. I saw no reason not to oblige her, and at seven thirty I found myself alone in the house. The boy was gone, too, off whoring or whatever it was he occupied his evenings with, and I picked up Homer, which I read until around eleven thirty, at which time I felt a need for companionship, even that of strangers. After determining that neither Mrs. Fenster nor her nephew had returned I descended, with the notion of returning to Schrafft's Biergarten.

The day's smoky fog still clung to the town, and the street's illumination was so diffuse it was impossible to distinguish clearly any object more than eight feet from the end of one's nose. Using the vague glow of the gaslights for markers I headed in the direction of Schrafft's, thinking foolishly that I might again see the young lady who had so captivated me the day before, and that this time I would have the audacity to approach her for a dance.

Before I had traveled three blocks a horrible, rhythmic wheezing sound burst forth through the brume, twenty feet or so distant, I thought. Alarming as it was, congested and panicked, it had also a comfortingly familiar quality; I nonetheless flattened myself against the wall and awaited its arrival with my fists clenched, and in a moment I saw a mass begin to take dark shape, moving unquestionably toward me. It waddled from side to side, suggesting an enormous razorback boar loosed inexplicably upon the metropolis, and I finally called out to it.

"Who's there?"

The sound stopped, replaced by a single sharp breath, and I heard a familiar voice call back. "I have a weapon," it cried, feminine and brash, old and belligerent. "I'm not afraid to use it, either."

"Mrs. Fenster? Is that you?"

"Mr. Sadlaw?" She came a little closer and her round, double-chinned face emerged from the mists, wide-eyed at finding me outside the house at this hour. I surmised that she had been running, if that was the word, from her sister's house.

"It's me. Would you care for an escort home?"

She nodded. "That would be most agreeable, Mr. Sadlaw."

I reversed direction and walked alongside her, slowing my pace to accommodate her short legs and limited wind. "And how is your sister? Improved, I hope?"

"Much improved, thank you." She seemed to take no pleasure from this, and we were silent until we reached our front door.

"I'll resume my promenade, then. Good evening, Mrs. Fenster."

"Good evening, Mr. Sadlaw."

She disappeared into the house, clutching her handbag. Before I started walking again I saw another silhouette wobbling in my direction. It was the boy, hopped up presumably and likely as not just back from a Market Street whorehouse.

"Evening, Mister," he said as he came to the door.

"Evening, Lem," I replied, and I resumed my walk.

SCHRAFFT'S WAS THE only illuminated structure on its block, its entryway a rectangle of washed-out, undetailed yellowish white. Within it was considerably quieter than the previous evening, and the fog spilled inside the enclosure to lay low about the floor. The bartender nodded at me. "Time for one drink, then I'm closing."

"Thought you were open all night."

"Some Saturdays we are. On a night like tonight we might

as well go with the laws and shut down at midnight." He spoke with a German accent, southern, I thought, though it was hard to tell in English.

He drew me a beer and I paid my ten cents, and he went back to his conversation with a red-faced gent whose hat had fallen off twice in the minute and a half I'd been there. There was no orchestra tonight, and no women to dance with anyway. The half dozen patrons scattered throughout the establishment were silent and grim-faced, and I wasn't overly sorry to be chased out.

Then without warning, six or seven feet away from me, one rummy stood halfway up from his bench and gave his neighbor a good sock in the jaw, with remarkable accuracy and speed for a man as deeply in his cups as he appeared to be. There was a clacking as of teeth colliding unexpectedly and the second man went down with a high-pitched cry of alarm and pain as the first man stood over him hard-eyed and panting. "That's for what you said about my wife, you damned hunk of dogshit."

"I didn't say nothing about your wife, you was the one saying things. All's I said was 'uh-huh' and nodded my head." Blood and spittle leaked from his mouth, and his lisp sounded like a loosened incisor or maybe a bitten tongue.

"Agreeing's the same as saying it," the first man said, and he stalked out the front door with the bartender's wary eyes trained on him.

When he was out the bartender stared at the fallen man, and when he had his attention he said simply, "Out."

"Hell, Jakey, I didn't do nothing, he just up and hit me for no reason."

"I said out, and if you want to come back tomorrow, you'll do what I tell you."

Grumbling, the defeated man rose, wiped his gory lip onto his filthy shirtsleeve, and shambled past me to the door. The smell of fresh blood played counterpoint above the deeper, dankish odor of his clothing, and the whole sad tableau evoked, not unhappily, memories of my own saloonkeeping days. I looked back at the bartender and saw that he held a billy club, slapping it into his left hand one, two, three.

"Some nights is nothing but trouble," he said. "You'd think charging a dime a glass we'd lose some of that trade."

I nodded and took another drink from my glass and then set it, two-thirds full, on the bar and walked away.

I SLEPT WITHOUT dreams, or without any that I could recall the next morning. Upon waking I made my way to the kitchen table where my morning papers awaited me, the *Bulletin* atop the pile as usual, and I sensed that Mrs. Fenster and the boy were waiting for me to react to it. The headline was larger than usual, a banner across the front page.

"Shall I read it?" I asked, and neither one responded. I began:

MURDERED IN HIS BED!

OUR PRESSMAN HIRAM COWAN ATTACKED ABED AT DOCTOR MARCY'S HOME AND CLINIC— DOCTOR MARCY THREATENED WITH A REVOLVER— HE IS CO-OPERATING WITH THE POLICE

Two China-men Were Seen Entering His House— They Arrived on Foot and Left the Same Way— Police Certain They Are Still in Denver.

Hiram Cowan, who was yesterday reported to be recovering from the wounds he received from an assassin outside the Silver Star Saloon, was last night shot and killed as he lay unconscious in the clinic of Dr. Hamilton Marcy. Dr. Marcy, having opened his front door to a pair of pigtailed China-men, was quickly held at gunpoint, blindfolded, and forced into a closet with his wrists tied before him. As he worked to remove his bonds he heard a pair of gunshots, and when he managed to open the closet door, which had been blocked shut with a chair, he found his attackers gone, and his patient dead with two shots to the brain pan. Morphine and other opiates were taken

> from the surgery, though whether robbery or murder was the motive for the deadly visit is undetermined. The doctor has been interviewed at length by the Denver Police Department and has furnished a general description of the apparently kindly Orientals to whom, thinking them in need of medical assistance, he opened his door last night; however, he told the *Bulletin*, he saw them but for a moment before his life was threatened and his eyes covered. Mr. Cowan, a valued employee of the *Bulletin*, leaves behind a wife and four children under the age of twenty.

"SORRY ABOUT YOUR father, Lem."

The boy looked confused, as if he couldn't imagine an appropriate response, and I asked him and Mrs. Fenster if they would require time off of work for the funeral. She shook her head no, and the boy, watching her, followed suit. I ate my breakfast, reading the rest of the *Bulletin* as I did so, and then took the papers with me to the privy.

My reading was not particularly conducive to the activity at hand, consisting as it did mainly of incitements to violence. In the *Rocky Mountain News* an article on the killing railed against the Chinese, noting pointedly that while Chinese women were not allowed to partake of stupefactants, many of Hop Alley's clientele were white women, and many of them middle class and respectable. Several papers that had previously ignored the story of the shooting enthusiastically ran articles relating cursorily the facts of the case, followed by lengthy editorial rantings over the Yellow Threat to Labor, Morality, and White Rule.

The boy and I did not discuss the matter while we worked that morning, and after lunch I sat up on the roof printing the previous day's portrait sittings. They were an eclectic mix: a homely debutante with her enormous mother, the latter poised to marry a penniless associate of her late husband's and the former bitterly opposed to the union (I gleaned this from their dialogue during the sitting, not one word of which was directed to me); an emaciated old miner who wanted a picture to send his brothers and sisters back in Pennsylvania; a newly married couple setting out for one of the mining towns where he was to make his fortune; and the elderly Chinese launderer. I imagined Hop Alley was in for a rough time of it tonight, with revenge-taking for the death of the pressman by men who never met him, with no concern for whether that vengeance was being visited upon Cowan's killers or their blameless compatriots. I wondered about Dr. Marcy's account of the theft of his morphine, for I had never heard of a Chinese hypo fiend; my understanding was that they used only opium, taken strictly by the pipe, and there were many hundreds more white morphine addicts in Denver than Chinamen altogether. I suspected he'd taken advantage of the incident to invent a theft that would cover his selling of morphine to hopheads, and I suspected further that the newspapers all knew this to be the case but didn't want to give up a chance to stir things up.

Upon descending to the gallery at one o'clock I found a man in a policeman's uniform seated in a stuffed chair there, smoking a cheap-smelling cigar. A more-than-usually sullen Mrs. Fenster, engaged in cleaning the glass cases, introduced him to me as Patrolman Heinecker of the Denver Police. I thought I had seen him a time or two, rousting drunks and harassing streetwalkers.

"I just had some inquiries for Mrs. Fenster regarding her brother's death," he said, looking quite pleased with himself.

"Brother-in-law," she corrected sharply, plucking at the hem of her apron.

He was clean-shaven and ruddy of complexion, though whiskey may have accounted for the latter. Two of the brass buttons of his blue tunic were undone, and his cap sat crooked on his head. "Mr. Sadlaw, do you know where this lady went last night?"

"She was here, as she is every night." I didn't quite understand why I felt compelled to lie, but it came out as naturally as the truth might have; I hoped Mrs. Fenster hadn't already contradicted me, and she raised her head and sniffed as though vindicated.

"Because you see, one of Doc Marcy's tenants downstairs from his surgery seen two old ladies come to call, both of 'em stout and short of stature, shortly after the arrival of the Chinee. The doc didn't see 'em, but the dead man's widow says to us, that sounds like my sisters, short and fat." He licked his lips and looked over at Mrs. Fenster, who stood with her plump arms crossed over her broad, shapeless bosom. "Just wondering if Mrs. Fenster had any thoughts on the matter."

"None at all," she said.

My imagination began to feed me little ugly thoughts about Mrs. Fenster's nocturnal outings, and her involvement with the old Mandarin, and I thought it best to distract the policeman from the similar thoughts that must have been percolating in his head. "Mrs. Fenster, I hope you haven't neglected to offer Patrolman Heinecker a little drop of something."

"I beg your pardon," she said, carefully separating each word in an exclamation of contemptuous disbelief rather than an apology or request for clarification.

"Patrolman, would you care for a glass of whiskey?"

He made noises as if to decline, then accepted. Beneath Mrs. Fenster's baleful eye I fetched a glass and the bottle and poured him three fingers myself. This might have been overdoing it but I sensed that was his usual dose, and he had a look of great peace as I handed it to him.

"That's awfully kind of you, Mr. Sadlaw."

"I'm told he was quite a brute, is that so?" I looked over at the boy, who watched the proceedings from the doorway of the studio, and at Mrs. Fenster, who would, I hoped, deny my claim.

"He was a sweet, gentle man, my sister's husband, and I'll not have you slandering him," she said to my great pleasure. She daubed at her eyes with a handkerchief.

"Still, what my friend Banbury—you know him, the editor of the *Bulletin*, where the dead man worked—Banbury told me he was a thug and a ruffian, with any number of people might have wanted him dead."

Mrs. Fenster wisely kept quiet this time, and the copper spoke next. "Matter of fact, we talked at some length with Mr. Banbury, and he agreed we ought to take a look at the two sisters. We said, Oh, we're going to do just that." My eye happened to be on Lem when the cop added, "He also thought we might have a word or two with the addled son, the one works for you." The boy slowly closed the studio door, and Heinecker remained oblivious to his presence. He was halfway through his glass and seemed quite content.

"Still, it's not much of a loss, is it? You're right, what we're hearing is what a mean, quick-tempered son of a bitch he was, begging your pardon, Mrs. Fenster, including how he cracked the boy's arm a few nights ago. Is that right? It was the boy's sister who told us that, a little tiny girl, and she seemed more relieved than grieving at her papa's passing."

"It's true, the boy's arm's broken."

"Is he here?"

"I sent him to the depot to pick up a parcel. Don't know when he'll return."

Heinecker knocked back the rest of the whiskey, and I would have offered him another glass but I didn't want to seem too eager to see him off his stride. "That's fine. I'll be back by tomorrow. Meantime, you keep an eye on the woman and the boy." He rose and headed for the door with his cap even more askew than before, and he walked with his fingers outstretched to meet the wallpaper. Going down the steps to the front door he had both hands on the left-hand balustrade, and he had to wait for a half a minute before opening the door to the exterior. The citizens of Denver were by no means unaccustomed at that time to inebriated policemen, but I hoped I had pushed his drunkenness to the point where a complaint might be made. Still, if he didn't return, one of his colleagues would, and before I spoke to Mrs. Fenster about the whole business I wanted to verify something.

I went to my room and opened the bottom drawer of my dresser. At its bottom was a bundle, wrapped not in the canvas sheet I had used, but in a piece of gunnysack. I placed it on the bed and unwrapped it; inside was a wooden case with a lock, and within that my long-ago trophy the Baby Dragoon. When I had put it away it was pristine, cleaned and oiled and polished and damned near as pretty as the day it left the Colt factory, or at any rate prettier than the day I took it off an insolent drummer in my Cottonwood saloon. Today it lay before me, cleaned after firing but hastily and not well, a whiff of Lucifer's domain lingering in its barrel. I placed it back in the case, wrapped it back up in the rough cloth, and replaced it in the drawer, then sat down for a long think about what sort of discussion I was going to have with my housekeeper.

Half an hour later I returned to the gallery and found her sweeping the floor. She stopped to face me, perfectly impassive, as though daring me to make a mention of her crime, or what she had used to commit it.

"Mrs. Fenster, in the future if you wish to borrow any equipment, photographic or otherwise, please be so kind as to ask. In addition, the Colt was not returned in the same condition in which it was borrowed, and I would be grateful if you would return such items to me directly rather than attempting to slip them unnoticed back into place, improperly maintained. Do we understand each other?"

"Yes, sir, Mr. Sadlaw," she said with more formality than was her habit.

The bell downstairs tinkled just then, and the old woman hastened down the stairs to answer it. I had a portrait sitting scheduled, and I went into the studio to make certain the boy was hard at work preparing the equipment and plates rather than cowering in the dark at the thought of the policeman come to arrest him and his auntie. I found him busily scouring the plates I had laid out, having seemingly forgotten Patrolman Heinecker.

That evening I took my horse and carriage out and rode to Golden with the Baby Dragoon in its case next to me. Though there was no way of proving that this particular revolver was the one that was used to slaughter poor comatose Hiram Cowan, I preferred not to have it in the house to tempt Mrs. Fenster, who might decide she had other scores to settle. Priscilla emitted a little coo of surprise when she opened the door and found me on her threshold with a box in my hands.

"Oh, a present." She reached for it, and I pulled it away.

"It's not. It's just something I'd like to keep here for a while if that's all right."

She was disappointed and didn't mind exaggerating it. "What is it, then?"

"Never you mind, just let me keep it here for a few days."

She pouted and turned away from me, though she'd already let me into her parlor. "I don't see why I should do anything nice for you," she said.

I handed her the laudanum bottle, which she accepted joylessly. "That's not the same as something pretty."

I slid my arms around her waist from behind and cooed into her ear. "I promise next time I'll bring you a little something, how's that, Cilla dear?"

"I surely don't know," she said, turning to face me and pulling away. I followed, assuming that we would be heading up the stairs, but she stopped me with a hand to my chest. "Not so fast, Mr. Sadlaw. Would you like some tea?"

"Tea?" I repeated stupidly. "Not really, thank you."

"Fine, you be seated and I'll be along presently." I sat on the canapé where I'd screwed her half a dozen times and tried to understand what she was up to. Perhaps I did presume too much; this was the first time I'd ever visited where there'd been any sort of activity intervening between the door opening and sexual congress. There was a book on a side table within reach, and I opened it. "*The Pilgrim's Progress*," read the title page; I hoped this was a family heirloom and not another sign that she'd found religion. To my great relief I found that it was a very old edition, and cheaply printed. Its pages, likely unopened since the middle of the last century, cracked and separated when I opened it, bits of their edges flaking onto the parquet, and guiltily I flicked them underneath the canapé.

After a few agonizing minutes she returned with a tray laden with porcelain teapot, cups, saucers, and creamer, and silver sugar bowl and spoons. She set them daintily down onto a small table and poured me my undesired tea, the very model of the genteel, sophisticated lady. She referred to me politely as "Mr. Sadlaw," and if not for the fact that the participants were an unchaperoned and possibly still-married woman and a man of decidedly murky matrimonial status, the tableau might have been one from any well-heeled Denver home of quality. Naturally this pastiche of gentility had the unintended effect of making me want to despoil her there on the hearth rug, and I suppressed the physical result of that arousal with difficulty as she made small talk about an imaginary husband and children, who would be joining us presently. That she might have been describing the actual family she'd left behind in Iowa did not occur to me then, nor did the thought that the distinctions between fantasy and reality might, for poor Priscilla, have begun to blur.

When she had tormented me sufficiently she returned the tray to her kitchen. "Now then, Mr. Sadlaw, you had something you wanted to leave here. Shall we go upstairs and find a good secure place to put it?"

I merely nodded and followed, docile as a randy schoolboy.

AN HOUR LATER it was dark and she lit a lamp next to the bed. "There's something I've wanted to ask you," I said as she ran her brush through her freshly disheveled hair.

"Ask away, though I may decline to answer," she said.

"Banbury says you're a fine singer."

"That's a statement, not a question, Mr. Sadlaw."

She stretched as she brushed, her back arched and her *poitrine* extended upward, and I thought that an observer might be forgiven for suspecting that she practiced this enticing pose in the mirror. "And that you accompany yourself very ably on the pianoforte."

"Another statement," she said with a sidelong glance that set my prick once again athrob.

"Why do you never play or sing for my benefit?"

The brush stopped and she set it down on her nightstand, then placed her right palm tenderly on my cheek. "Oh, my poor dear. You are a darling, but Mr. Banbury takes care of me in ways that you don't, and it wouldn't be right for me to share my musical gifts with anyone else. You do understand, don't you?"

I wanted to laugh but worried that she might bludgeon me. "I ought to tell you something," I said, feeling for a moment quite fond of her. I knew I oughtn't, really, but I gave her an accounting of Banbury's plan.

She was quiet, and she didn't cry as I'd been afraid she might. "That son of a bitch," she said under her breath. "If he thinks he can cast me off like that."

"What'll you do?" I asked.

"I'll do what he makes me," she said, and I didn't ask her to elaborate.

"According to Banbury, you could easily sing on the stage."

She gave me a look of unvarnished, venomous umbrage. "Take to the stage? Is that your opinion of me, after all we've shared?"

"I meant the legitimate stage, my dove, nothing low or unworthy of you." I made a mental note to ask around Denver about positions for experienced seamstresses. Then impulsively I said something, regretting it even as I heard the words coming forth from my tongue. "Why don't you move in with me? There's plenty of room, and Mrs. Fenster does all the housework. We can tell people we're married."

"Well I'll be goddamned if I'll pretend to be anybody's wife that lacks the balls to actually marry me," she said, and I thought maybe I'd go down and get her a couple of spoonfuls of laudanum. She softened quickly on her own, though. "Oh,

Bill, I don't mean it's not a sweet thing to offer. I'll just have to think about it. I'm used to my solitude, you see."

"Suit yourself," I said with no small amount of relief.

She got up quickly and dressed, and hurried down the staircase to the parlor, where I heard her remove the tea tray to the kitchen. I put the case on the top of her placard whose small filigreed ledge obscured it from view. When I returned to the parlor she was seated on the canapé. "I suppose you'll be going now?" she said, and I thought I heard in it an unprecedented plea to stay and pass the evening with her.

"Expect I will be," I said, unable to imagine what we would do now if I were to remain; play cards, perhaps, or draughts, or sing songs. The prospect of inviting a woman to move into my house, when all we'd ever done together was screw, struck me now as extravagantly foolish. Without making any further reference to my offer I stepped outside into the cold night.

"Remember," she said as I stepped onto her front landing, "next time you owe me a present."

I tipped my hat to her and got into my carriage and headed in the direction of town, troubled by my lack of self-restraint. How could I have imagined that a conjugal residence with laudanum-addled Priscilla could end in any manner other than pure disaster?

I had long since established to my own satisfaction that I was not well-suited to domesticity. Back in Kansas I'd abandoned my sweet, randy Danish wife, Ninna, to live in town and run a saloon, leaving my farm and Ninna to the ministrations of a hired man. And when I left Kansas, with the law at my heels and the blood of Maggie's husband on my conscience, I'd brought Maggie along, she whose beauty and intelligence were far beyond what a feckless, loafing philanderer such as myself merited; and yet within three months of our settling down in Greeley I left her, too, ostensibly to prospect for silver but in fact with the singular goal of getting away from the Greeley Colony and its prim, teetotal utopians, whose number now included my own Maggie, no longer just playing at being my legal wife but believing it herself.

I rarely contemplated the unhappy period of my leaving her, temporarily and then for good, but my rash proposal to Priscilla brought that gloomy time back to me, and I had to remind myself for the first time in a long while that I was well off in her absence.

FIVE

An Earlier, Equally Ill-Conceived Proposition

I had lasted but four months at the Greeley Colony. By February I had lit out into the hinterlands with a meager set of supplies, a mule, and an overstated sense of my chances, and without Maggie's blessing. My brief incarnation as prospector was notable for its lack of success in a time when fortunes were being made in what was still the Colorado Territory.

The end of it came in April of 1874 when, after two luckless months, I came across a crudely built spruce cabin along Williams River. By the looks of the cut wood at least two or three seasons had passed since their felling, and the shanty's roof was just about to cave in from an accumulation of snow. I undid the leather thong that kept the door fixed shut—whoever had been here last had shut it from the outside—and entered. Inside the windowless room, illuminated only by the light streaming behind me from the doorway, I squinted against the dark and detected a whiff of decay in the closed air.

As my eyes grew accustomed to the dim light I spied upon an old G.A.R. cot the cadaver of a prospector, withered as a month-old apple and wearing a shit-stained union suit. His decease had preceded my arrival by several months, and apart from the befouled long johns and the cot everything of use or monetary value had been made off with by persons unknown, most likely other prospectors, who had at least done him the kindness of lacing the door shut with that leather thong to keep scavenging animals out. Or perhaps the thieves were guilty of more, and obfuscation their intent; the wretch's permanently open jaws and sunken eyes revealed nothing about the manner of his death.

I had abandoned my own camp three days previous and was heading in the general direction of Georgetown. It was tempting to stay here for a while, given that the cabin already stood, but it seemed clear that its previous occupant hadn't prospered here. And so for some reason not entirely clear to me at the time, but which in retrospect seems to me a base sentimentality springing from a recognition of myself in the poor dead failed prospector, I removed the spade from the pack on my mule, Abelard, and began digging a grave.

If you've never tried to dig a grave in the Rockies in the dead of winter (and believe me when I say that this particular April qualified as such), I will warn you off of it here and spare you the effort. It was a miserable job, with Abelard staring at me with his big, black, round, wet left eye as though this confirmed every suspicion he'd had of me.

I managed three feet in depth and congratulated myself on a job well done. At this stage of his decomposition the prospector had very little smell and I doubted that those scavengers would now show him much interest; however, having laid him in the earth and covered him, I set about covering the grave with stones to discourage any especially ravenous beasts that might disturb him.

I was about to make my way onward but decided one last sweep of the cabin might be worth my while. A superstitious mind might conjure that this was the miner's grateful ghost prodding me onward, with a view to his treasure not being lost forever, for in the far corner of the crude structure I spotted a patch of earth that was slightly higher than the rest, though its builder had done a reasonably good job of leveling the rest of it. Intrigued, I took the spade back off of Abelard and began digging.

A foot or so down I hit something. I pulled from the earth a leather pouch, and dandling it in my hand I estimated its weight at about half a pound. I loosened the drawstring, and my heart filled with visions of another Omaha-sized windfall. From within I pulled a single daguerreotype and a trio of tintypes, all four framed identically. The daguerreotype was of a couple, about sixty or seventy years of age, their manner of dress suggesting material prosperity around the time of Millard Fillmore's presidency. The tintypes were of more recent making; the first featured a boy of about eight and a girl several years younger. The second added their mother, a sweet-looking woman who was nonetheless far from pretty, with squinty eyes and a nose like a carrot. The third tintype added to this grouping a tall fellow whom I took, though neatly dressed, clean-shaven, and uncorrupt, to be our prospector.

I placed the photographs beneath the stones marking the grave, and for just a moment thought about keeping the leather pouch, since it would be perfectly suited to holding gold dust. I said as much to the mule, who gave me a look that seemed even more contemptuous than was his habit, and I was overwhelmed with a sense of my own ridiculousness, and a sentimental urge to return to the settled life I had briefly enjoyed with Maggie.

And so I walked Abelard for two days to a shabby new town whose name I never bothered to learn, where I traded him for a night's food and lodging (our parting was not without its element of pathos, but mules are fickle creatures and he took quickly to the tavernmaster in whose possession I had placed him). In the morning I bought a coach ride to the town of Golden, a miserable trip I shared with a plump and talkative widow named Mrs. Miles, whose entire family history was known to me by the time we arrived at our destination the next morning. Alone in the interior of the coach, she felt no inhibition against detailing the shortcomings of her youngest daughter's husband, which included uncleanliness, insobriety, and a violent temper. He also had the gall to move her daughter to the dirty little burg from which we had just departed, there to operate a barbershop which the widow had staked him. This selfsame fellow had cut my hair upon my arrival and given me my first decent shave since I'd left Greeley, and I had found him a sullen and disagreeable character, so rash in his handling of his scissors that I feared for my ears.

She also recounted in lurid detail the scandal caused in 1836 when her maiden aunt ran off with the just-married son of a local minister, who at twenty-two was seventeen years her junior. In the aftermath of the pair's departure it came out that this aunt, though unmarried, was hardly inexperienced in the ways of love, and that many a lusty young man in their Iowa town had learned the truth about the world under her tutelage. The minister's son, dissatisfied with his new bride's amatory skills, then convinced the spinster to run off with him. I concurred when the widow asserted that the offspring of churchmen are often impious and untrustworthy sybarites, and when we parted ways at the depot she invited me to call on her at her home. I was tempted, not least because of her sly implication that she and her wayward aunt were kindred souls. I hadn't know a woman's embrace in some months, but an illicit liaison seemed the wrong tack to take, seeing as I was on my way back to Maggie with an eye to reconciliation, and I regretfully declined the invitation. (Hedging my bet, I did promise that when and if I returned to Golden, I would call on her.)

After spending fifty cents on a meal of ham, biscuits, and gravy that a billy goat might have spurned, I wandered the town looking for a spot for a photographic studio. I had nearly fifty dollars left of the Omaha windfall, very little of which Maggie and I had spent beyond securing our position at Greeley and purchasing Abelard and the contents of his saddlebag. By midafternoon I had found an ideal spot, a storefront with a second-floor skylight, and a room in the rear that would be easy to modify into a darkroom. I negotiated a rental price of fifteen dollars per month with the landlord, a rheumy and morose fellow who seemed not to care in the least whether he had tenants or not.

The next day I started for Greeley. I expected to meet with a certain amount of disdain and even hostility from the home guard, among whom I had been an unpopular figure owing to my undisguised contempt for the colony's aims and most particularly for its founder, Mr. Meeker, a man whose enthusiasm for industriousness in his subjects was matched only by his own fierce disinclination toward labor.

Yet the looks I got as I wandered into the colony's main public square were more incredulous than hateful. It had been snowing all day, big evanescent flakes that vanished on contact with the ground, and those who passed by me, hunched forward in their threadbare winter coats (the colony, alas, had never attained the state of prosperity promised by its founder), regarded me as they might have done a Saint Bernard striding on its hind legs. A mousy old squab of sixty or seventy, sporting the remains of a black bonnet in a style fashionable around the time Zachary Taylor was president, wisps of white hair peeking crazily from its edges, hissed at me as I passed.

"Unclean thing," was what I understood her to say, though I may have been mistaken. It was only at the sound of her voice that I recognized her as the wife of the Reverend Dunwoody, both of them kind souls who had previously treated me quite kindly.

Upon my arrival at my former home I was made to understand the surprise on the part of the denizens of the colony. "I told them you were dead," is what my dear Maggie told me once she'd regained her composure and stopped pummeling my chest with her little rosy fists. "Do you think I wanted it known I'd been deserted?"

To be truthful, this hadn't occurred to me at all. And it was only half true that I'd deserted her, seeing as how I'd left with the intention of returning a wealthy man and luring her away from this dreadful place. I'd supposed, of course, that I would have to resort to a bit of honeyfuggling before she broke down and wept tears of joy at my return, but this degree of vitriol surprised me. I hadn't ever seen her this put out and I very nearly despaired of the carnal reunion I'd been rehearsing in my mind for so many months.

"Your notion that you can fly off, without my blessing, for months and months and never even let me know you're still breathing . . . "

Here I interrupted her, normally a perilous endeavor, but I had a legitimate objection. "Did you imagine there was a telegraph office where I was?"

She slapped me, rather harder than a person might think possible just looking at her. At that moment I thought I'd never seen her looking so beautiful, her long, regal throat exposed and flushed pink as her cheeks, but I sensed that if I expressed that thought it would come off as pleading, and so I feigned an intention to leave.

"All right, then, I'll move along." I put my hat back on.

"Go," she said.

I opened the door, expecting her to weaken, but she said nothing as I exited and shut the door behind me. I heard the latch click shut as I walked away.

There was a boardinghouse above the dry goods store, and as fortune would have it one of its tenants, Norville Queenan, had just been kicked in the belly and then, as he fell, in the head by a dray horse he'd overworked. Now he lay prostrate in the back room of Dr. Galway's infirmary, with very little hope offered for his eventual rehabilitation. I remembered him as a particular favorite of Meeker's, a humorless New Englander who believed in the colony as fervently as he had previously believed in Joseph Smith's Mormon revelations and William Miller's eschatological ones. His disillusionment with those religious movements—in 1844 he had sold his farm and given away all his money in anticipation of the Reverend Mr. Miller's Advent, and after it didn't arrive Norville never recaptured the relative wealth of his youth—had led him to seek an earthly utopia, and he talked often and openly about how Meeker's notions differed from those he'd abandoned, because they were based on science rather than the supernatural.

That night, lying in Queenan's rope bed, I heard precious little. The colony was a very tranquil place at night, having no saloons or even a beanery, and most of its citizens worked so hard at farming that they returned home exhausted in the evening and retired upon finishing their evening meal. Those who didn't work on the farm—Maggie, for example, sewed, and I had worked as photographer and editor of the weekly newspaper—were expected to follow the same schedule as the rest of the colony.

Despite the quiet I had no urge to sleep. I had seen in Maggie's eyes that afternoon no inclination to welcome me back, no desire to forgive me my absence—or, more precisely, no desire to forgive my disobedience in setting out away from home. I had also been taken aback when the operator of the boardinghouse told me to watch out for a Swede named Thor Sundkvist, who had been bird-dogging Maggie ever since she let it be known that she was now a widow. (Which of course she was, though not my own; how odd, I thought, that she'd forgiven me shooting her actual husband, but couldn't excuse my going off to prospect.)

I had, of necessity, maintained a life of fidelity since my departure (or one of celibacy; under the circumstances they amounted to the same thing). The notion that Maggie might not have made my stomach hurt, although I knew the town well enough to be certain that physical intimacy between an unmarried man and a supposedly widowed woman in such a place would require a level of discretion and stealth and chicanery worthy of a stage magician. The lamps may have gone out by eight in the evening, but eyes were still peering out those windows, and malicious tongues were the norm there.

I did finally manage to drift off, though, and slept fitfully until around three in the morning when I awakened to the sound of my door latch creaking. I reached under the bed for my Baby Dragoon, which I'd had the foresight to load in case Mr. Sundkvist got it into his head to eliminate his competition. I pulled back the hammer and growled.

"Who's that?"

"Who do you imagine," I heard a soft voice say, and then my Maggie quietly disrobed and climbed into Norville Queenan's bed with me. "I'll do my best to be quiet," she said.

OUR REUNION HAPPENED quickly, too quickly for the satisfaction of either of us (remember, please, that I had been alone for eight or more weeks, with only Madame Palm and her five daughters for such comfort), and as we rested waiting for the occasion for a repeat performance to arise we spoke softly. She was ready for me to return, but only if I would take a job on the farm, as there was no need for a photographer there (never had been, really). This had been the state of affairs when I left, and I was no more ready to take her up on it now than I had been before. I didn't argue, but I told her I wanted to go to Golden.

"My illusions are dead as regard prospecting," I told her. "But there's money to be made from them that succeed. I've leased a studio in Golden, and if all goes well there, I might open one in Denver."

Did I believe as I said it that the notion of a comfortable living—prior to taking up company with me, after all, she had lived the life of a wealthy woman—would affect a change in her outlook? Yet that had been my ostensible motivation in leaving the colony to prospect for gold, even if a desire to escape the strictures of Greeley had played a large role therein. And since my return I had been reminded of certain aspects of Maggie's personality that had also pushed me toward a life of solitude, aspects I had allowed myself to forget during my months of trial.

"All right, then," she whispered, sounding quite as cold as she had earlier at our—her, rather—cottage, and she extracted herself from my embrace, slipped from between the covers, and dressed.

"If you've a change of heart, stop by in the morning. Otherwise, be out of the colony by midday or I'll have you charged with desertion and who knows what else."

At that she left as quickly as she could while maintaining a discreet quiet, and I fell asleep rather quickly, having come to a conclusion the moment she was out of the room.

When morning came I descended, having slept strangely well, and tucked into my grits and the single egg offered per boarder at the breakfast table, and wondered whether there was a correlation between the colony's poor performance and its inability to properly feed its members. The local blacksmith, a reformed drunkard named Clyde MacPherson, ate with me, the other boarders having wakened earlier.

"I never reckoned you being dead," he said. "You never did much take to Meeker's notions, did you?"

"Not much," I allowed.

"How'd you come to land here, then? The little lady?"

"Something like that."

"I don't mind telling you she's an awful pretty thing."

"That she is."

"But truth to tell if I was still a drinking man, I wouldn't want to be here. Chief advantage it has for me is there's not a drink to be had for twenty miles in any direction." His nose was still pocked and scarred from his days as a soak, and he had once told me that his missing lower incisors had come out one night while he was passed out in an alley, yanked by a dentist he'd sucker-punched after an argument about the pope of Rome.

I told him about my encounter with Mrs. Dunwoody, and he assured me it was nothing personal on her part. "She's lost her reason, like as not she didn't even know it was you. Poor old reverend, she started hearing voices and saying things that weren't very much in line with proper Methodist thinking."

He finished off his breakfast and took his leave. "You'll be leaving, then?"

I told him that I would, and alone at that.

"I wouldn't worry about her, she's been right about distraught since you've been gone. Just let her know where to join up with you once you get settled and you can lay odds she'll find you."

I shook his hand and told him I hoped that was true, but that I doubted it. Before I left town I pilfered a sheet of paper and an envelope from the unattended room of the boarding-house's operator and borrowed a pencil from MacPherson.

Dear Maggie,

I am sorry that our reunion was less than happy. If you wish to return to me, you have but to proceed to my photographic studio at Washington Avenue and 12th Street in Golden. If you do not wish to do so, I do not hold any grudge against you. Do **not** *ask me to rejoin you in Greeley.*

With great affection,

Your Bill

In July, happily ensconced in my new home and studio, and doing good business, I received a letter from her. Since I had instructed her to come to Golden if she wanted to reconcile, I presumed that the letter was a plea to return to Greeley, and so I burned it. I burned the one that came the week after that, and all those that followed—their frequency increasing until, by the first week of August, I received one every other day—until they stopped, abruptly and for good, the second week of August.

A month or so later, when I had decided to move the studio from Golden to Denver, I was seized by remorse and returned to Greeley hoping to persuade her to come with me; she was long gone, however, with no forwarding address. And that, I thought, was it for me and Maggie, two stubborn souls who spent a bit less than a year in one another's company.

SIX

Hop Alley Aflame

These thoughts of love's labors lost had put me into a decidedly melancholy state on my drive back to Denver, and I was shortly distracted by the smell of smoke and the visual signs of a conflagration. The flames, or rather their glow, reflected into Denver's heavily particulate atmosphere, were visible well before I reached town, and having no special attraction awaiting me at home I put the horse and carriage away and began wandering in the direction of the fire.

Some distance before Hop Alley the sounds of screaming and shattering vitrines could be made out, and at Twentieth and Market, where normally I would have expected to find any number of harlots advertising their wares on the sidewalk, there was not a soul to be found excepting Miss Mary Dolan, late of Boston, who remembered me from our last meeting. Her pasty face glistened oily in the light of the moon as she took my arm in a gesture of great familiarity.

"Look at that, Sean, fireworks, just like you promised."

"In a manner of speaking, Miss Mary."

"So I'm thinking to myself, maybe we ought to stay right here in Denver if there's fireworks same as in Boston."

She still clung to my arm as if we were about to take a stroll somewhere, though we stood rooted to the spot. "I'm not Sean," I said.

"Sure you are," she said with a fond laugh. A cry rose from the disturbance, a lone, sorrowful yell soaring over that of a crowd, and a shot was fired. Then the crowd's voice swelled as the solo voice sharpened and then cut itself off.

"Any idea of what's drawn the crowd over there," I asked her, though I expected I knew the answer.

"I want to tell you something, Sean, it's only fair and just that you know before you take me on as your wife. Since my arriving here in Colorado I have done some things of which a good girl mightn't be proud."

"I'm sure it's all right." I was seized by a desire to return home and forget about the fire and the ruckus, read about it in the newspaper the next morning.

"No, Sean, you don't understand." She squeezed my arm. "I've sold my virtue in the mining camps and here in the city. Oftentimes for the mere price of a drink or a dose of morphine."

"That's what priests are for," I offered, assuming that she was at least by birth a member of the Church of Rome.

"What about our babies yet to come, Sean? How can I cradle them, knowing what I done?" She looked on the verge of tears; those yet-to-be conceived, imaginary babes were quite real to her, and feeling my pity about to dissolve into melancholy I took my leave, promising to visit her again soon.

As I PASSED through an alleyway leading to the Chinese Quarter I was nearly bowled over by a shaven-headed youth, moving with the speed and intensity of purpose of a tomcat with a string of sizzling petards tied to its tail. At the end of the alley he turned northward, and before I had turned back around a gang appeared at the mouth of the alley in pursuit. Several of them carried lanterns, and as they approached the man in front yelled to ask me which way he'd gone.

"Southward," I said as they passed, and was gratified to see that to a man they turned in that direction at the alley's mouth, not a one of them troubling to glance over his shoulder to see if I'd lied.

I exited to Seventeenth Street to a scene of violent depravity. Laundries stood in flames as the fire brigade strove to contain the damage, and small groups of young Chinamen brawled with those of young whites, though the numbers in these groups were uneven and mostly favored the white boys. Amidst the fighting ran individual rioters, some of them holding aloft articles looted from the various establishments of the quarter; several brandished opium pipes and what appeared to be snuffboxes, and others ran about laughing hysterically wearing comically ill-fitting clothes. That last annoyed me, imagining as I did that my own shirts and trousers might be among those being paraded mockingly through the pandemoniac scene before me.

I saw a pair of blue-coated Denver Police patrolmen, one chasing a young Chinaman who eluded him with ease, weaving in and out of the madding throng and finally disappearing into the same alley from which I had just emerged. The other stood guard over six youthful Chinamen who sat manacled to one another, displaying the same sullen affectlessness as the young one who'd accompanied the old laundryman to my studio several days before. One of them was an exception, exhibiting extravagant rage and provoking violence from the patrolman. He snarled an indistinct but doubtless foul epithet at the copper, who replied with a blow across the face from his billy club, and at the instant he struck I recognized them both: the victim was the very nephew of the launderer, and his attacker was Patrolman Heinecker, still drunk to judge by his slow, stumbling carriage. The youth struggled not to show the pain and managed to convert the rage on his face into a semblance of the stoicism he'd shown before.

He saw me looking at him and, recognizing me, gestured with his head to the north. The streetlamps there had all been extinguished, and I saw no animation there at all. Squinting, however, I perceived that a man hung at the corner of Wazee from a lamppost, the light of which had been extinguished; to my shock I thought I saw the man moving slightly. Getting closer I could distinguish the unconscious face of the elderly uncle, alive and slowly strangling. Though the crowd had lost interest in the hanging I was unarmed and didn't dare risk incurring its wrath by cutting the old man down, so I hastened back to the spot where Patrolman Heinecker stood guard of the nephew and his compatriots.

Heinecker's face was the picture of cocksure drunkenness, and I thought it a wonder his weapon hadn't already been taken off him. He looked at me as though we were old friends, and he made no effort to stop me as I grabbed his stick from his hand and brought it down on the side of his head. He did look surprised and confused, and he started to say something; his finger was pointed at my face as if trying to place it when I hit him a second time and he started to fall. I didn't hit him a third time, for fear of killing him or harming him permanently, which I suspected I might already have done; he was down for the moment in any event, and I took his revolver from his belt with no resistance, cursing myself for having left the Baby Dragoon at Priscilla's.

I returned to the lamppost. Whoever had slung the noose over its crossbar had left a short ladder on the ground, and I propped it against the post and ascended with my jackknife open.

I had sawn halfway through the hemp, horrified at the wet rattling sound coming from the old man's constricted throat, when someone shouted.

"Hey! You son of a bitch, you can't cut down our chink! What the hell are you doing that for?" A barrel-chested fellow with various unruly strands of wet hair plastered across his forehead rose from a prone position and half crawled toward me. His shirt was drenched and so were his trousers, and I noted for the first time that this northern part of the street was all mud, and that several of the buildings were smoldering in the darkness.

"Someone moistened you, looks like," I said, with the amiably distracted tone of a man interrupted in the performance of an uninteresting task. I hoped he was drunk enough to be sidetracked and that I could leave the sidearm stuffed in my belt.

"Fuckin' fire brigade," he said. "Ought to have been quicker to put out the fuckin' fire and not so quick to hose us down."

"Is that what they did?" My jackknife was duller than I wished, and the cutting was slow.

"Hell, they ran out of water and had to go back for more before they even started on the fire. They's lucky we din't fuckin' pull 'em off that wagon and give 'em some of what we gave this here chink." He squinted, and his thoughts returned to the matter at hand. "And what the hell you think you're doing, anyway, cutting him down? He ain't even dead yet."

"City ordinance," I said. "What can you do?"

"Son of a bitch's gotta pay for the white man got killed the other night. Killed him in his bed's what they did, his sickbed, even, and somebody's gonna have to pay for it."

There was little to be gained, I thought, by explaining that if someone did indeed have to pay, then in fact it was my trusty old housekeeper that belonged at the end of the noose, rather than any member of Denver's Chinese populace. Seeing that the conversation could serve no further useful purpose, and hoping to prevent him calling to his comrades to the south, I continued sawing and with the other hand pointed Patrolman Heinecker's Colt at the man's balls.

"He's coming down, and if I hear another sound out of you, I'm going to ventilate your ball sack, you understand?"

I thought I might have to make good on the threat, but at the sight of the gun barrel pointed at his middle he gave a disgusted little wave and ran yelling across the muddy street to crash his fist into a window. It was hard to see but I heard the smashing of the glass, followed by a bellow of pain.

"Ahhh, son of a *bitch*!"

Then I heard him slumping down onto the planks of the sidewalk as the final strands of the rope parted and the old man fell into a heap at the foot of the lamppost, and I regretted not having plotted an easier descent for him. Except for the drunk with the bleeding fist, who sat weeping and cursing me and the old man both, my action had gone unnoticed; there was no other objection when I picked the man up and slung him over my shoulder to a nearby building, one of a number that had been spared destruction by the fire brigade's muddying of that part of the street.

A door opened unbidden as I reached it and the magus and I were pulled into its dark interior amidst a cacophony of voices muttering and whispering hoarsely in what I assumed to be Mandarin.

"The old man's still alive," I said.

"You go," an angry voice shouted at me from the darkness.

"You hear? He's still alive. I'm going to go over and get a doctor I know," I said, though to be honest I thought even Ernie Stickhammer might require the persuasive qualities of Patrolman Heinecker's revolver to get him to tend to a Chinaman in the middle of the night, with a riot in progress scarcely half a block away.

"No doctor. Chinese doctor. You go now."

My eyes had begun to adjust to the light of the room, and I saw that the old man had been removed, and that I was in the company of six or eight Chinese; remarkably, all of them looked as elderly as he or even older. One of them opened the door and another shoved me out.

The door shut quietly behind me, and I saw the drunk sitting in the same spot as before, mumbling to himself and still making sad sounds. I didn't think he'd seen me exiting the building, but as I passed by him on my way away from the disturbances he looked up.

"Say, you son of a bitch, wha'd you do with our chink?"

I put the revolver to his head and pulled the hammer back. "Go home," I said, and he rose to his feet and stumbled away from me, babbling incoherently, and I looked over at the group of young Chinamen. The old man's nephew looked at me impassively, and a different patrolman had replaced Heinecker, who still lay on the ground where he had fallen. Thinking about that as I headed back home I hoped that meant I hadn't killed him.

SEVEN

Hop Alley, Laid Waste and Captured on Glass

I had not thought much of the girl I'd left behind to go to war since returning from that war under somewhat questionable circumstances and finding that she had married another man and died in childbed, which indicated, I suppose, that my love for her was not as eternal and pure as I'd thought. That I was secretly relieved to be free of her does not make me proud, but the fact that it had been years since she'd crossed my mind must have been a sign that our union would have been an unhappy and impermanent one.

On the night of the riot, though, I dreamt of her. That she was alive in this dream and that we were standing on a Denver sidewalk was all that I recalled upon awaking, and that I was shouting, "I *deserted* for you," so loud my throat was raw as I sprung from bed, winded and swinging my fists at the empty air. I would not sleep again that night.

The house was silent but for the ticking of the grandfather clock in the foyer, which showed the time to be after four. I dressed myself and roused Lemuel.

"What the hell?" he asked.

"Wake up, lad," I told him. "Time to earn your pay." He lay there, bleary, and I did most of the work loading up the chemicals and the dark tent, then packing up the stereographic camera.

"What's all that for? How are you figuring to take pictures at night?"

"Won't be nighttime for much longer." Before we got to the front stairs Mrs. Fenster met us in the foyer, candlestick in hand.

"You're awake," I said.

"Fancy sleeping with you howling like you were. Where are you going in the middle of the night?"

"Going to teach the boy how to work in the field."

"Put all that down," she said, "and at least get you some breakfast. Sun won't be up for hours, and there'll be no use in him slopping muck onto the glass before that."

With some reluctance I allowed as how she was correct, and the boy and I sat at the table. Neither of us said a word until his auntie brought the coffee in.

"I suppose you're wondering what we're off to record in the light of the dawn," I said.

The question hadn't entered his mind, and now that it was raised he remained incurious and indifferent, but I told him just the same, explaining what we were about to document, and he nodded his understanding.

"I seen some of that last night. There was burning and yelling, and some of the harlots wanted to go take a gander at it and some of 'em wanted to bar the doors."

His aunt betrayed no reaction to that last statement as she brought in a plate full of bacon fried to black, and we didn't speak as we ate. When we were finished I sent him around to the livery for the wagon, which we loaded up and drove to Hop Alley.

The morning fog made the residual smoke from the inferno hang low, and blended with that from the city's hearths the air at the site of the riot was acrid and damp. Hopping from the wagon near the streetlamp that had served as the old magus's gallows I found the drunk who'd tried to keep me from cutting him down. He was unconscious, smeared with the mud he lay in, and he reeked of various effluvia. I touched him with my foot to see if he was alive; he grunted but didn't wake.

The street was unpopulated and silent, its calm so different from its normal frenzied activity that I wondered whether every single Chinese in town hadn't been taken into custody. Above me, though, someone quietly closed a second-story window and latched it, and behind another window opposite that one I spied a face glaring at me in the faint foredawn light; as our eyes met it withdrew, ghostly, into the darkness of the room.

I decided to start with some of the burnt-out buildings across the street from the one I'd taken the old man into, and by the time I had set up the camera and dark tent the sun was rising. As it crested the horizon it cast a dramatic ray on a charred interior beam of the building before me; on its ruined facade was a large sign with Chinese characters running down its left side and the word LAUNDRY to their right. Its interior appeared to be a total loss.

Once three views of the ruined laundry had been committed to glass I ventured inside of it. The flames had already been put out by the fire brigade when I'd arrived that night, and the blackened timbers had grown cold. There was that particular sharp, smoky smell of an abandoned campfire, and of the laundering facility itself very little remained but some galvanized tubs full of water and ash and burnt wood. I took down a sign from the wall and laid it artistically on one of those tubs as though it had fallen there, and setting up the tripod I yelled for the boy to bring me some fresh plates.

When I had done with them Lem took them to the dark tent as I poked around the room searching for another angle bright enough for a sharp image. I thought I had found one when the boy returned empty-handed.

"There's a whole bunch of Chinamen standing over there 'cross the street looking awful mad," he said.

Stepping outside I saw that this was so, and rather than risk starting another riot I ordered the lad to begin packing up. There were six or seven of them, of varying ages, and they stared at us without consulting one another or indicating what their intentions were. They did not appear happy at the sight of me traipsing through their ruined quarter like a Roman tourist at Herculaneum, and presuming what's more to take pictures of it, and for a moment I felt an unaccountable sense of shame. I made a great show of moving the crate over to the wagon, and they watched as we packed up the dark tent and shoved everything onto the back of the wagon. Their eyes were still on us as we rode away, and they looked no more content for seeing our receding backs.

I LIKED THOSE pictures more than any I'd made in a long while, and I printed up a set of proofs that very afternoon. By eleven in the morning the sun had burned off the fog, and not much later I sat up on the roof enjoying Old Sol as they came up. I had Plato's *Last Days of Socrates* with me, but I had read it a dozen times before and wasn't overly annoyed when the boy broke my concentration.

"It's that one-armed fellow again, got a package from back east." He hesitated before continuing: "He mentioned he'd like you to make it quick this time."

"Tell him I'll be with him presently," I said, and the boy, looking nervous, went back downstairs. I examined the prints with greater care than was really called for, then set about a lazy inspection of the four corners of the rooftop. Having determined that they remained structurally sound and properly tar-papered I lazily mounted the ladder and descended into the foyer, where the disrespectful son of a bitch sat fuming.

"I'm sure you think it a fine joke, keeping me waiting."

"Beg pardon?" I said, all innocence.

He shoved a package in my direction. "That's eighteen dollars and thirty-five cents, payable upon delivery."

"What's it consist of?" I asked, knowing perfectly well that it contained a six-inch lens I had ordered eight weeks prior.

"How would I know what's in it? Look at the sender's name."

I squinted and shrugged. "McAllister Photographic Supply Company, Philadelphia. Never heard of them."

"All right," he said, and he tucked the box under the stump of his missing arm and strode toward the staircase.

"Hold up, there," I called. "I'll pay."

"No, sir, Mister, there's obviously been some kind of mistake made." He was at the top of the stairs now, turned my way, smirking. "Good day, sir."

I did need that lens, and I was willing to let him win the game at this point. "All right, I was having you on. Now give me the package."

The smirk became a sneer. "I'll by God eat the eighteen dollars myself before I'll let you have it."

I reached out for it, thinking to snatch it from its perch between stump and rib, and he beat me to it with his remaining hand, the stump flailing like a dodo's useless wing. "Sorry," he said.

"See here, a joke's all it was."

His face was getting redder, and the scars showed white against it. "If you think costing me time on my route is a joke, friend, you're sadly mistaken." He stood there at the top of the steps, holding the box like a baton. It was a foot long, wrapped in brown paper and tied with twine and stamped FRAGILE, and he made as if to toss the thing down the stairs.

I rushed him, and instead of throwing it he brought it across my jaw with great force and a loud crack. The pain was sufficient to bring me down to my knees. "Eighteen dollars and thirty-five cents, please," he said, and I rose to my feet. My left hand to my jaw, I was preparing to sneak a right uppercut when Mrs. Fenster came out of the kitchen to see what the trouble was.

"Imagine what the folks will say when they hear how you beat up a one-armed cripple," she said, wiping her hands dry on her apron.

"Who's a cripple?" the fellow said. "Anyway, I hit him."

She gave me a warning glance and turned on her heel, and chastened I held my hand out for the package. Reluctantly he gave it over.

"Hey," he said when I opened my jackknife and cut the twine. "You have to pay for that first."

"I'm checking for damage before I accept delivery," I said. "If you don't like that, you can go back and tell your employer how you broke the damned thing smashing it across the customer's mandible."

The lens appeared to be in good condition, brass barrel undented and all elements intact, so I paid the man, who left without another word. My jaw had begun to throb, though oddly it wasn't quite at the point where he'd hit me, and probing the teeth with my tongue I pinpointed the trouble spot at the lower left bicuspid. I hoped the pain was temporary and wouldn't require a trip to the dentist's for an extraction, for I had all mine still and was rather proud of the fact. When Mrs. Fenster served her midday meal I avoided the left side except for the bread pudding, and I thought it might be all right.

COME THE TAIL end of the afternoon I had made a goodly number of prints of the Hop Alley views on albumen paper, and I ordered the boy to begin mounting them. I needed to make the trip to Golden that evening, but not for the usual reason. Not only for that reason, in any case; I had been brooding all afternoon over the prospect of taking over Priscilla's maintenance. In the light of day it seemed a nightmarish proposition, an invitation to catastrophe, and it was only fair to tell her so now, if not in those precise, indelicate terms. Probably she'd already decided against it anyway, but in either case I had to retract the offer before its potential acceptance.

I was too weary to drive the buggy, and so I treated myself to a train ride to Golden. When I descended at the tiny depot the sun was sinking, and the air quite a bit chillier than it had been down in the city. When she opened her door, dressed like Denver's finest society matron right down to the hat on her head, she made no comment about the hour, to my relief.

"Shame on you, Bill, I thought you mightn't come. Step inside."

As I did so she explained that we were expected back in Denver at the Charpiot Hotel for a reception Ralph Banbury was giving for his daughter's engagement.

"I don't think I'm dressed for the occasion, Cilla," I said.

"I've some of Ralph's clothes here, and they'll fit you close enough."

"Are you truly invited?" I asked.

"Of course," she said, taking no offense. "Ralph and I had a long talk about things. He's awfully relieved about your offer."

That seemed a promising opening for the hard news I

wanted to deliver, but my tongue remained still in my head as she handed me an engraved card:

Mr. and Mrs. Ralph Banbury
Invite you to join them for a Reception
to Celebrate the Engagement of their
Daughter Gertrude to Mr. Harold Neville
Seven o'clock Friday Evening the 26th of April 1878
in the Ballroom of the Charpiot Hotel

I wondered why I hadn't received one of these, and I saw the envelope it had arrived in; it was addressed to me at the studio, and not to Priscilla.

"You took this from my mail," I said.

"I saw who it was from, dear heart." She touched my cheek with her gloved hand with great affection and squeezed. "Surely it was meant for both of us."

Wriggling out of this was going to be a more complicated affair than I'd imagined, and when I thought it over it seemed to be all the fault of Ralph Banbury. I didn't see any reason we shouldn't go to his reception; any embarrassment he might experience would be richly merited.

We exited. At the same moment as it occurred to me that it was the first time I'd been in her house without screwing her, I realized that we had no carriage and no convenient train into Denver, and no available train for the return either, and

I led her to the livery stable, where I hired a Concord buggy and a handsomer nag than I normally would have been willing to pay for. We said little as we bounced our way into town, and Cilla looked so content to be at my side I felt monstrous; I even doubted my resolve at one point and wondered how bad it would be to settle for a life with her, taking pictures of Denver's illustrious and unknown and having her waiting for me *à poil* at the end of every day, as voluptuous and perverse as Messalina herself, with only bed, board, and the bottle necessary to keep her happy.

We rode first to the studio, where I hurriedly put on my formal evening attire, and then straight to the hotel, where I turned the buggy over to a bellman, and from there we proceeded to the ballroom.

With its walls festooned with crushed velvet and ten-foot-long tables laden with every sort of delicacy known this far west, and doubtless a few appearing here for the first time, the presence of a throne and England's queen herself would not have seemed incongruous. We were met at the door by a liveried footman, and though I was famished, Priscilla insisted on immediately joining a reception line where the parents of the bride- and groom-to-be stood with their offspring accepting the congratulations of what looked to me like every single mining tycoon in Colorado, their wives and mistresses and an array of lesser figures, from Banbury's fellows in the newspaper trade to the mayor of Denver and, if I wasn't mistaken, the governor himself. A small orchestra played a waltz to which many of the partygoers were dancing, and waiters circulated with bottles of champagne.

I watched Banbury shaking hands and making light and brief conversation with his guests, looking as miserable as I had ever seen him look, even though his eye was substantially improved, to the degree that it was completely opened and sported only a mild discoloration.

"Look at that bitch," Priscilla said in too loud a voice. "So he's quitting me for her?"

I looked around, wondering who she was talking about and astounded that Ralph would invite his new mistress to such an affair, and then I saw that she was referring to, and staring at, Mrs. Banbury. Once I'd caught sight of her I couldn't take my eyes away either. The extravagance, verging on the garish, of her costume—a silk dress of sea green, with pea-green accents, and a hat decorated with bright emerald parrot feathers—only served to accentuate her homeliness, which would not have been so remarkable in a woman dressed in a more modest fashion. The daughter was no beauty either, with wide-set eyes and snaggled teeth, but her face betrayed a sweetness of character that her forbidding mother seemed at first glance to lack altogether; the doughy fellow next to her blushed to hold her hand and, despite Banbury's claims of greed on his part, appeared genuinely consumed with affection for his fiancée.

Though we had not yet taken plates for the buffet, the slow-moving receiving line passed by several tables, one of which contained a plate of hors d'œuvres that no one was watching over. Surreptitiously I took a tiny pastry from the plate—a tiny mushroom turnover, by the look of it—and held it behind my back, then scanned the room to see whether I had drawn any disapproving looks; satisfied that I had not, I popped the thing into my mouth and bit down, enjoying a fraction of a second's joy at its warm savor before letting out a horrible yell and doubling over, as the left side of my face erupted in pain as sharp as any I'd ever felt in my life. The generalized ache of the morning was gone in an instant, leaving only that violent throbbing in my jaw where the one-armed messenger had smashed the box. I did attract a few stares then, including that of Muriel Banbury, who did not seem pleased, but the room was noisy and the orchestra had started a new number.

One partygoer who had failed to notice my distress was Priscilla. We were nearing the honorees, and she clutched her purse and smiled fixedly. Still riveted by the blinding flashes of fire that coincided with each heartbeat I no longer worried that she would make some inappropriate remark to one of the Banburys, and when I heard her talking to Muriel I was only halfway interested in the exchange.

I did see, however, that midway through whatever Priscilla said to her Muriel's face froze and she yanked her hand away and turned toward me. "And you would be?"

"Shadlaw," I lisped, terrified of making any sound that would bring my upper and lower mandibles into contact with each other.

"Our tenant." She seemed genuinely surprised I'd made the guest list but recovered quickly enough. "The photographer. I see. I'd like to have Mr. Banbury speak to you about arranging a bridal portrait for Gertrude."

"I'gh ghe gherighted," I said. Priscilla had passed the bride and groom, who looked offended and puzzled respectively, and was just reaching Banbury, who looked as uncomfortable as possible, and glared at me in frank anger.

"Please feel free to call on him at the offices of the *Bulletin*," Muriel said as I saw Priscilla open her handbag, into which she stuck her right hand very slowly. I thought Banbury was about to complain aloud to me; his mouth was open and he was looking straight at me when we both heard a familiar clicking sound; his eyes followed mine to Priscilla's hand, which, as the prescient reader will have guessed, held the Baby Dragoon, its hammer cocked and ready. Before either of us had a chance to grab it from her it fired.

The cellist stopped almost simultaneously with the shot, throwing the first and second violinists off tempo for a few beats until they too quit in confusion, leaving only the brave violist to stab gamely away at Herr Mozart's quartet for another full measure. Ralph was on the floor with a bullet in his chest and Muriel bent over him, screaming, her hand slick with his blood.

"Bargain for me, will you, you son of a bitch?" Oddly I was very conscious of being very, very hungry as Priscilla swung the Colt at my face, and also of her considerable physical attractiveness, which her rage only accentuated. I heard her say "I will not be treated as a goddamned mule—" and then the barrel made contact with my jaw. I remember a flash of pain more horrible than the last one, and going down toward the carpet with the first stirrings of arousal, and then nothing.

EIGHT

A Brief Sojourn in the Hoosegow

Opening one eye I determined that the prickly substance beneath my head was straw. The room in which I found myself was dark and suffused with myriad odors so delicately intermingled as to be unidentifiable, though I thought I detected a leitmotif of rancid urine over long-unwashed clothing and chronic mildew. My evening clothes were wet in spots.

"What the hell's this place?" I said, looking around at a dark room about eight feet by ten, with nine other men crowded into it.

"Denver Shitty Jail," lisped a man with as ruined a face as I'd seen since the war, his malformed nose competing for attention with a mostly missing upper lip.

What could I have done to get myself locked up, I wondered momentarily, and then the throb in my jaw brought first one thing to mind, then seven or eight more that, scrutinized in the light of day, might have earned me a trip to the jug. I sat up and sniffed, and identified another scent among the many, an unpleasantly familiar one.

"I smell rotten flesh," I said, and as sick as I felt I feared it might be my own.

The deformed man's neighbor, an ectomorph with the matted beard and demented eyes of a prophet, gave a short bitter laugh. "Goddamn City Jail's nothing but the back room of the Butterick Meat Market."

I was fortunate enough, then, to have been arrested in my unconscious state by a city policeman and not a county peace officer, who would have removed me to the county jail, a serious place of incarceration. The city facility, on the other hand, was a makeshift pen mostly intended to hold drunks and short-term felons with little motive for evasion. My cellmates were four Chinamen, including the nephew of the magus I'd cut down from the lamppost, and five white fellows. The prophet and his scarified companion and a third man, a hog butcher by trade, had been arrested during the riot. The other two wouldn't say what had landed them in stir, but the first was a sorrowful drunk, his bender wearing off quickly and leaving him desperate for a cupful. Though the second was seated, I would have guessed his height at six and a half feet tall at least, and he was as thick side to side as a chest of drawers.

The five white men sat on the floor on the left half of the cell, and the Chinese on the right, and there was a certain amount of grumbling from the left half when I first crossed the cell to the right to speak to the old magus's nephew. The Chinese didn't much like it either, and one of them rose to his feet in a threatening stance until the nephew said something to him with a gesture in my direction. His compatriot sat back down with no more friendliness showing on his face than before, but the nephew bade me sit. He introduced himself as Fong, without specifying whether that was his first or last name, and said that he believed his uncle had survived. Unsolicited, he also offered up his opinion that Mrs. Fenster had persuaded the old man to provide two advance men to distract and overpower Doctor Marcy while she murdered her brother-in-law. The two men who accompanied her (without, according to Fong, stealing the doctor's opiates or anything else) were ignorant of her mission there, though Fong's uncle surely knew why she needed the doctor out of her way.

I returned to the other side of the cell, where I spent the morning striking up no friendships and cultivating no allies. The three rioters, having failed to fold the remainder of the cell's Caucasian population into their clique, spent their day talking amongst themselves and until the turnkey arrived at noon with tin cups and a bucket of corn gruel their colloquy on the various and sundry character deficits of the Irish, the Jews, the Catholics, and the Chinese were the only words spoken aloud in the cell, apart from the souse's mostly incoherent whimpering. The gangly jailer, so bent and arthritic he walked nearly sideways like a crab, dropped the bucket on the floor and threw the cups onto the shit-stained straw without a word, then scuttled back out, ignoring my demands to know for what I was incarcerated.

"Are you deaf as well as crooked?" I shouted at the door.

The three rioters laughed. "You won't get much out of him. He don't care for our class of character," the prophet said, dipping his cup into the gruel.

After they ate the foul corn—I felt too ill to partake—the door opened again and a pair of policemen entered with a defeated-looking man in civilian clothes. It took me a few moments to recognize the silhouetted figure as that of Officer Heinecker.

"This the man what took your iron off you?" the first copper asked him.

"That's him," Heinecker said, looking me sadly up and down.

"What's the charge?" I asked the coppers.

"Accessory to murder, as well as unheeling a duly charged officer of the peace," the second one said, sounding amused.

"Banbury's dead?"

"He will be soon enough."

"I want to see my attorney."

"If wishes was horses, then beggars would eat." They led Heinecker off and locked the door again.

"Say," the prophet piped up. "You took that copper's gun off him?"

"I needed it."

"When'd you do that? On the street?"

"During the riot."

"The Chinee riot? Then what the hell you so friendly with that chink for? Don't you know they killed a poor old man in his sickbed?"

I sat down without answering, and as the others gulped their swill Fong leaned over to me and spoke very quietly.

"Five prisoners escaped this same jail six months ago. Broke bars out of the window." He nodded at the window; the bars had been reinforced with what looked like cement.

"Might be worth a try," I said.

The prophet dropped his empty tin cup and rose. "I want you to stop talking to that son of a bitch."

I glanced at him without answering, and when I turned back to Fong I noted that his companions were watching the group with concern, though Fong was careful to ignore them.

"Did you hear me? Come on over to the white man's side or I'll crush your skull like a fuckin' melon."

I turned to find that the three of them had risen. The one with the ghastly scars was laughing through mostly toothless gums as though Christmas was coming. I stood and faced them, and I supposed I'd have to drop the prophet first and hope the other two would be intimidated into backing down. Lacking confidence and feeling weak as a babe from fever besides, I was trying to calculate the likelihood of Fong and his comrades coming to my aid when the gigantic, speechless man on the floor rose to his full height and width—even more massive than he'd appeared when supine—and spun the prophet around with one big paw, then cuffed him solidly across the face with the other. I thought I heard the smaller man's nose crack, and he collapsed like an abandoned marionette onto the pissy straw.

"Gott-dam tired of listening to you," the giant said, and then he returned to his seated position on the floor. That was the last we heard from the rioters until the evening meal, when the prophet tried to elicit assistance from the turnkey.

"That big Dutch son of a bitch knocked me down," he said.

The turnkey shrugged painfully and spat at the ground. "Be glad he don't fancy fucking you in the bargain." He left another bucket of corn gruel, and after he went off for his own meal we decided to try our luck first with the bars, while the others disinterestedly concentrated on their unappetizing meal.

I rotated one clockwise, then counterclockwise, and it gave easily in the concrete the jailers had haphazardly poured after the last escape. The bar was long, however, and though we could move it vertically two or three inches it wouldn't come out far enough to allow our egress. After watching us for a minute the giant grunted, dropped his cup, and drew up to his full height, then moved to the door and started pounding.

"Jailer! Dem crazy chinks has done and caught the straw on fire!"

I looked over at Fong, who looked puzzled for a second and then let out a scream of such convincing pain I thought he was truly injured. "I'm on fire! Help!" he shouted, and I joined my own voice to the chorus. Fong yelled something at his friends in Chinese, and they commenced screeching as well in their own tongue. Only the drunk and the three rioters kept eating, looking puzzled by the cacophony.

"Pipe down," the prophet said. "Ain't nothing burning."

The giant reached down and backhanded him ever so gently across the face. "Shut it or I'll break it." The prophet shut it, his eyes glistening.

I heard the turnkey coming then, keys jangling, yelling for us to hold on, and when the door opened the big man gave him an uppercut that lifted him into the air before depositing his skinny, bent frame on the ground.

He looked around and then scowled. "Ain't no goddamn fire in here." He started to stand and then he was looking straight at a fist the size of a ham hock. "Now hold on a goddamned minute." The rioters had stopped eating, though the drunk was taking advantage of the confusion to drink his muck straight from the bucket, and spilling the stuff down the front of his gray shirt, from which he scraped bits of wet corn with his grimy finger, which he then licked more or less clean.

Fong slipped out the door and returned with a set of wrist irons. He took the keys from the jailer, who was quietly making predictions about our speedy capture, and he chained the poor fellow to the bar we had failed to remove.

He looked sadder than he did angry. "You sons of bitches are going to get me fired," he said as we filed out of the room calmly.

Outside on Thirteenth Street we could hear him yelling immediately. The giant wanted to go back inside, but Fong stopped him. "Always outside the jailhouse people hear yelling."

The giant nodded. "Best ve split up now," he said, and all concurred but the three rioters and the drunk, who were headed straight for the nearest saloon, the Rusted Nail. The last I saw of them they were whooping in harmony as they entered.

NINE

AN ANGEL'S MINISTRATIONS

By the time I had made my way through the dark streets to my studio the fever had worsened considerably. Opening the front door, which no one had seen fit to lock, I had to fight back nausea at that old familiar smell of graveyard detail and the Benders' charnel pit, and for a moment I wondered whether I wasn't delirious, for I could think of no rational reason for such a smell to permeate my entryway, unless Mrs. Fenster had died during my absence and gone undiscovered until now. An eerily faint orange light was barely discernible in the upstairs foyer, and I imagined I heard the muffled weeping of women.

Atop the stairs I was greeted by the macabre spectacle of a veiled quartet of ladies, dressed in mourning and quietly lamenting. Black crêpe bunting had been draped all about the walls of the foyer, and though candles were burning throughout the room no lamp was lit, and it was impossible to make out any of the faces beneath the black lace veils. At the center of the room on a makeshift catafalque lay a figure so small I took it for a child at first, until its features, distorted by two or three days' lifelessness, resolved in my mind into those of my poor stunted assistant Lemuel. I presumed, then, that these were his aunties and his mother.

I bowed in the ladies' general direction, as the stoutest of them rose huffing to her thick feet. "Didn't have any way to ask for your permission," she said.

"Mrs. Fenster?" I pointed at the still form. "What happened?"

She gave me an odd look. I attributed the pinching of her nostrils to the general stench in the room until she opened her mouth. "I shot him, as you well know, with your own gun."

"Lemuel?" I asked, stupefied at such a claim.

"Lemuel's over there." She indicated a corner of the room near the gallery where the boy sat on a wicker chair with a look of bovine contentment on his imbecilic features. Looking over at the body on the slab I reconsidered its concave eyes and its lips drawn tight to reveal its uneven dentition; even in that state, these were clearly the mortal remains of a man of forty or fifty, and I understood that its slight resemblance to my own idiot assistant was a family one.

Mrs. Fenster had raised her veil, and I noted to my surprise that she herself had been weeping. "I'm surprised to see you carrying on so about Cowan," I said.

She sniffed with some force, snorted, really. "He was my brother-in-law for an awful long time, Mr. Sadlaw, and wasn't always mean."

I nodded, and sniffed myself. The smell was powerful, and I wondered aloud why he hadn't been put underground.

"What with the riots and your lady friend, plus a fire in a boardinghouse, the undertakers is all busy with the better sorts of stiffs, and Hiram's been moved to the back of the line with the paupers."

"I understood the *Bulletin* was going to pay all the funeral expenses."

"With Mr. Banbury dead the paper ain't paying for planting nobody but Banbury." She studied my face and scowled. "You're not well."

"I'm not," I allowed, and I sat down in a narrow armchair that sat against the wall. The pervasive tinge of corruption in the room exacerbated the effects of the fever, and a sweat had broken on my brow.

"You could do with a bite to eat, I'll wager."

Oddly, despite the ferocious stench in the room and my queasiness, I did feel hungry. I hadn't eaten since the fateful hors d'œuvre at Banbury's reception.

"Come on into the kitchen, I've kept the door shut and the smell's not bad in there." I followed her waddling form through the door and found that the odor was, indeed, much diminished. She offered me first a biscuit from a tin. I bit into it with relish, and though it was a tasteless thing it was a pleasure to swallow. On my second bite I forgot myself and bit down with the left side of my jaw, and presently howled with such force that when I fell off my chair Mrs. Fenster's three sisters burst into the kitchen to see what was the matter.

The pain was momentary and was replaced quickly with a foggy dreaminess as my housekeeper and her three veiled sisters clucked over my prostrate form, arguing about what was the matter with me. The fever seemed to rise back up in me with great speed, and I began wondering who was under which veil. I supposed that one sister was the pressman's widow, that another was Mrs. Fenster's murderous accomplice, and I wondered whether the third wasn't the sister Mrs. Fenster had gone to visit ten years prior, from which trip she returned to kill the faithless Mr. Fenster. They seemed to be swimming above me in some sort of thick but transparent fluid, and their voices weren't entirely clear to me either. I managed to point at my mouth.

"Tooth," I yelled.

They picked me up and, as one, carried me through the house to the sound of rustling cotton. They babbled incoherently as they laid me out on my bed, and Mrs. Fenster lit the bedside lamp. She made some sort of pronouncement, and they all gasped at it.

Mrs. Fenster disappeared for a moment, and one of the sisters removed her veil. To my astonishment she was a lovely woman of perhaps forty years, and bore only the most tangential resemblance to my housekeeper. She mopped my brow with a handkerchief, muttering soothing words to me, and I began to feel the shameful stirrings of an erection. At that moment Mrs. Fenster returned, and at her signal the two still-veiled sisters each took hold of one of my arms. The lovely widow straddled me indecently at the waist, then grabbed my lower jaw and, simultaneously, my forehead. I was at once aroused and terrified, and as Mrs. Fenster approached me from the side I screamed, certain these were the angels of death, come to take me to hell. This arranged very well for Mrs. Fenster, who deftly inserted the pliers she had gone to fetch into my mouth and yanked powerfully once, twice, and thrice. At three I lost consciousness, aware that the fractured molar had slipped from its moorings.

I awakened on several occasions without truly regaining full consciousness; just enough to remember hearing Mrs. Fenster talking to a police officer about the reason the dead man was still in the foyer, and about her theory of where I had gone.

"He was here just long enough to pack his grip," she said, "and then he lit back out, never to return. He said he was headed for Ohio, where he has folks."

There was also a hubbub at one point because the idiot boy had punctured the hand of the dead man with a fork, stabbing it to the makeshift catafalque and laughing maniacally. That may have been a fever dream, however.

And then toward the end of my delirium I was brought into something akin to consciousness by the extremely pleasant sensation of some sort of warm wetness at my groin. Upon opening my eyes I found one of the sisters bobbing her head up and down at my waist. I must have let out a gasp because she looked up, disengaged her mouth from my prick and, using her right hand to keep the black veil from her face, smiled most pleasantly at me.

It was the widow Cowan herself, and the muted daylight that showed through my drawn curtain revealed her to be, if not the beauty I'd deliriously imagined the other night, a reasonably handsome woman nonetheless, despite a right eye with a tendency to wander, and a nose that had been broken and badly set. She seemed not at all embarrassed to be surprised in such an act. "This is by way of thanking you for being so kind to my boy all these months." She slipped her mouth back around my cock and, lowering the veil, resumed bobbing. As she did so the border of the veil rhythmically grazed the skin above my groin, and though I was somewhat bothered by the smell of her husband's putrefaction in the other room the overall sensation was pleasurable. I drifted back into a dream-state and she became a dozen women one after another, starting chronologically with Mary Harding and proceeding forward. When a Kentucky lass whose name I couldn't remember metamorphosed into my abandoned wife Ninna I was taken by surprise but, oddly, not displeased, and it was into Ninna's hungry gullet that I discharged a day or two's worth of ejaculate. I opened my eyes again to find the widow wiping her lips with a handkerchief in a demure manner.

"My name's Henrietta, but they call me Hennie," she said, and I slipped back into contented sleep before I found the words to reply, aware that I was recovering and anxious to be going.

A DAY LATER I sat upright as though just waking from a satisfying night's sleep, and called for Mrs. Fenster.

"Do you want me to fetch you some soup?" she asked when she came in.

I took a whiff and nearly told her no, famished though I was. "Not to be indelicate, but when are the undertakers coming?"

"For Hiram? They came and got him yesterday. He's planted like he belongs." I must have looked dubious, because she added, "That's a smell that's going to linger for a time. You'll have to be leaving anyhow."

She handed me a *Rocky Mountain News* from a stack that had been growing at my bedside and pointed at an article on the front page:

BETRAYED BY THIRST

ANOTHER ESCAPE FROM THE CITY JAIL

The Mayor Has No Explanation.

Four of Ten Evaders Caught in a State of Inebriation, Four Chinese and Two White Inmates Still At Large. One is Accomplice of Banbury's Murderess.

This was not the lead article, however. My old chum Banbury claimed the top of the page:

EDITOR'S ASSASSIN CALLED "MADWOMAN"

District Attorney Vows: *"SHE SHALL HANG."*

Oft-Wedded Medusa's Motives in Killing Beloved Editor Are No Doubt Political.

"Where's my grip?" I swung my legs off of the bed.

"Packed," Mrs. Fenster said. She went to fetch me a pitcher and a bowl for washing up. It wasn't as bad a job as I'd have expected after a jailbreak and several days abed; the widow Cowan had sponge-bathed me while I slept, having detected at close quarters an offensive odor distinct from the cadaver's.

Once I had washed, shaved, and dressed I took a survey of the studio and gallery. There was no possibility of hauling the inventory or equipment, nor of having them shipped, and once again I was faced with the prospect of running out of a place I had adopted as my own; at least this time I had the opportunity to pack a few articles of clothing. I told Mrs. Fenster and Lem they could have it all in lieu of severance pay.

"Rent's paid here until the end of the month, so get it out before then. Or perhaps you could come to an agreement with Mrs. Banbury and stay."

She snorted. "And who'd make the pictures? I can't. The boy's barely got the smarts to pour that stuff onto the plates and dip 'em into the chemicals, he doesn't know how to have people sit, or what to make a picture of."

This was hard to dispute, and the boy nodded, unoffended at his auntie's assessment of his capacities. I began to scratch out a list of photographers and dealers in photographic goods, and a rough approximation of what I thought my gear might bring.

She balked when she saw the amounts on the page. "That's too much for severance, Mr. Sadlaw. How's about I send you half the proceeds?"

"Don't know where I'll go and if I sent word when I got there, it might be intercepted."

She nodded. "I might keep some of the chairs and the sofa for myself. And the pianoforte," she said.

"I didn't realize you played."

She seemed almost wistful as she gazed upon it. "I don't but they're nice to have in a parlor."

I hied to my bedroom where I lifted a floorboard and took

from its hiding place a roll of bills. Eighty dollars; not a princely sum but more than I'd had when I fled Cottonwood, and this time I left behind me no loved ones, only a business and some objects of monetary value. In a decade hardly anyone would remember I'd been through, much less regret my absence.

TEN

Exeunt, Pursued by a Bear

I considered heading eastward, but between my Ohio upbringing and my experiences in the war the region held few happy associations; besides, I'd never seen the Pacific and had heard that it was bluer and colder than the Atlantic, and that seemed sufficient motivation for a westerly trajectory. For thirty dollars I purchased an old roan mare, since I didn't want to board the train in Denver, and rode her to Cheyenne, in Wyoming, passing along the way the Greeley Colony. Its pious and shiftless founder had lately died an ignominious death in the western half of the state at the hands of the Utes, the finest horsemen in the West and possibly the world, whom he had stupidly tried to turn into dirt farmers. I didn't stop to inquire as to the current prosperity of the colony's residents.

Arriving in Laramie I sold the mare at only a five-dollar loss, which I counted as a bargain. I hadn't bothered to name her and she seemed unruffled by our parting. The next day I boarded a train on the Union Pacific bound for California, and as it hurtled westward I pondered whether I ought to adopt yet another new name or keep Sadlaw for a while. As William Ogden of Kansas I was wanted for murder, a crime for which there exists no statute of limitations and for which I was liable to be extradited and hanged if found out; but as William Sadlaw I was wanted, as far as I knew, only by the city of Denver, and only as an accessory. It takes time and effort to acclimate oneself to a new name, and as Sadlaw had been my maternal grandmother's maiden name, and as I had been fond of her as in my childhood, I felt inclined to keep it.

Before we'd crossed out of Wyoming I caught the attention of a pair of children, a brother and sister about six and eight years of age respectively. They climbed over the banquette in front of me and began to stare at me, for want of any more compelling diversion. Their mother sat a few rows ahead of me, apparently asleep, and they took my silence and failure to acknowledge their presence as a sign that I wanted to be friends.

"We're going to Stockton in California," the girl said. "It's where our papa's family live."

"He's dead," said the boy.

"Throwed out of a window," said the girl, eyes wide with wonder.

"By a man he did business with. He ruined him, the man said."

"That's a shame," I said.

"Just as well. Our uncle says Papa would have gone to prison anyway if he hadn't been killed."

The girl's eyes widened further. "The policeman who came to our house to tell us said he broke every single bone in his body, including his skull and all his fingers and toes."

Her curls were all done up in pink ribbons, and both she and the boy wore clean and well-made clothing, suggesting a social station that would have sustained irreparable damage from a felony conviction.

"Where are you coming from?" I asked.

"Chicago," said the boy.

"Our papa worked at the Board of Trade. It's an awful lot of money he's supposed to have stolen."

"Might as well hang for a pound as a penny," I said.

Their mother, having roused herself and found her babes gone from her side, arose and made her way back to us.

"I'm sorry, sir, for my children. Come back and sit," she ordered them.

"Not at all, madam. I enjoyed our interview."

She favored me with a weary smile tinged with sadness and affection for her tots. "They're without much to do on a long ride like this." She had a round, pretty face with a sore on her lip that I hoped hadn't arisen from another of her late husband's vices. She was flushed and slightly sweaty from her nap; four stray tendrils of wet hair stuck to her forehead, which bore the imprint of a railway pillow's braided ornament.

"Lovely children," I said, feeling an unwanted twinge of pity for her.

"That is true," she said without joy or enthusiasm, and she took each child by the hand and trudged back up to their own banquette and took her seat again with an unconscious sigh.

AFTER A ROUGH night's sleep I awoke to find the train slowing on approach to the promisingly named town of Ogden, Utah, and the mangy conductor limped through the car announcing a stop of one hour.

"Is there a restaurant at the station?" asked the widowed mother as she shod her drowsy charges.

"In a manner of saying so," the conductor said without looking her way. He had white sideburns thick as squirrels' tails and a pair of pince-nez with only one lens. "Man that runs it's an old army cook. I wouldn't eat there if I valued my health."

THE WIDOW DECIDED to stay on board and feed her children from a stack of stale-looking graham crackers wrapped in waxed paper, but I was anxious for a stretch and soon found myself seated at a long counter and addressing the old cook. A good many of my fellow had descended, but only five of us sat down in the cramped dining room to eat. While I ate a pair of fried eggs that were a shade greasier than I preferred, the ill-shaved, slovenly cook grumbled at length about our conductor, with whom he had some sort of continuing grudge involving the cook's sister, long deceased.

"Nothing wrong with them eggs, is there?" he asked.

"Nothing," I said, eager to avoid a long discourse.

"Sure there ain't. He runs down my food every time he passes through. I wrote a letter to the president of the railroad himself, and all I got back was a letter from a secretary telling me to go fuck myself. Pardon my French, ma'am," he said to a large, dainty woman dressed in lavender who affected deafness and continued working on her plate of ham. "I wouldn't let my sister Sal marry him on account of he was a Methodist, and Methodist and Baptist don't mix."

"You're not Mormon?" I asked.

"No, sir. Primitive Baptist."

"I can't help but notice you don't serve coffee here."

"They won't let me. I don't mind, though, that's one place where I agree with them. That and tobacco and alcohol. Nothing but badness. And I have seen things on my travels, Mister, that would make you turn away from all those things.

After the war I spent ten years in California, from Oregon on down to Mexico, and the entire state was full of such vile wickedness it would make you rebuke those intoxicants too."

"I've never been, but that's where I'm headed."

"Beware, friend. A wicked, wicked place."

I nodded. As I hadn't yet chosen what part of the state to start my new life, I thought this man might be as good an oracle as any to determine where to light. "And what would you say was the worst part of the state, Mister? South or north?"

"Well, sir, you pose a difficult question in many ways, for there are pockets of blight and sin up and down the state like pustules, each bad in its own way. But I'll tell you, I've never encountered a worse or baser bunch than those in San Francisco. Debauchery and vice, and all in the name of mammon. It was gold that cursed the town, sir, and the more gold they brought up from the ground, the more Satan smiled."

I nodded and thanked him and finished my eggs and paid. I left him a whole nickel for a tip, grateful as I was for his advice, and as I boarded the train I found the idea growing on me: *William Sadlaw Photographic Gallery, San Francisco, Cal., Sittings by Appointment Only.* By Friday I'd have arrived, by Monday at the latest I'd have leased a studio and equipment, and I would be back in business.

My troubles would be over.

ACKNOWLEDGEMENTS

All of the cities in this novel—Denver, Golden, Omaha, Greeley—are figments of my imagination and differ from their real-life counterpoints as my whims dictated. For a great account of Denver in this period, I wholeheartedly recommend "Hell's Belles," by Clark Secrest (University Press of Colorado). Rick Lasarow, MD, long ago consulted with me on the behaviors of certain characters. Finally, sadly, without my friend Cort McMeel's encouragement this book never would have been finished. He left us way too soon.

ABOUT THE AUTHOR

Scott Phillips is the author of *The Ice Harvest*, *The Walkaway*, *Cottonwood*, *The Adjustment*, and *Rake*. He was born and raised in Wichita, Kansas and lived for many years in France. He now lives with his wife and daughter in St. Louis, MO.